REASONABLE FACSIMILE

AN ANTHOLOGY

BY

DEL STAECKER

K. S. LUKE

CLIFFORD L. CARTER

MARK FLEISHER

SANDRA MILLER LINHART

REGINA D' SCRIPTURA

DUSTY FACINELLI-JANISCH

LIONHEART GROUP PUBLISHING
PUBLISHED IN THE USA

REASONABLE FACSIMILE
AN ANTHOLOGY
APRIL 2025 ~ FIRST EDITION

FOR INFORMATION REGARDING PERMISSION, EMAIL LIONHEART GROUP PUBLISHING: PERMISSIONS@LIONHEARTGROUPPUBLISHING.COM

COVER BY SANDRA MILLER

PAPERBACK ISBN: 978-1-938505-77-5
HARDBACK ISBN: 978-1-938505-78-2
LIBRARY OF CONGRESS CONTROL NUMBER: 2025935288

10 9 8 7 6 5 4 3 2 1

PUBLISHED BY LIONHEART GROUP PUBLISHING, LANDER, WYOMING, USA

PUBLISHED IN THE USA ~ ALL RIGHTS RESERVED.

VISIT US ON THE WEB AT WWW.LIONHEARTGROUPPUBLISHING.COM

LIONHEART GROUP PUBLISHING IS AN IMPRINT OF LIONHEART GUILD, INC; A 501(C)3 NON-PROFIT

Dedication

To all who have dared to dream, and to those who have found beauty in the unexpected...

To the ones who have built their lives brick by brick... And to those who have learned to dance in the rain—this is for you.

May your journey (whether it mirrors your hopes, surpasses them, or is only a *reasonable facsimile*) be filled with moments that remind you of your strength and grace.

And as you walk this path, remember: kindness, to yourself and others, is the quiet miracle that makes every life extraordinary.

Be kind. Always.

Reasonable Facsimile

Table of Contents

THE SECOND DAY

K. S. LUKE

On the first day of the rest of my life
I had a double-scoop cone of huckleberry ice cream
And laughed while it dribbled down my arm;
Weeping in creamy, purple streaks as if shocked & saddened
To find itself exposed to the desert sun.
And so, on the second day of the rest of my life
I had to work out—twice.

On the first day of the rest of my life
I stoked my education with a breezy 'Click' to enroll
And danced around an imaginary bonfire; plotting a white-hot course
Through branching neurons, and emerging theories of the brain
That would be enlightening, revealing, healing.
And then, on the second day of the rest of my life
I had to study—for hours.

On the first day of the rest of my life
I serenely planted my garden with radishes
And kale, and heirloom tomatoes rooted under organic mulch.
I let fly the ladybugs, and released the earthworms like a mother;
Protective, as they tunneled away from wings & heat.
And so, on the second day of the rest of my life
—I weeded.

INTRODUCTION

REASONABLE FACSIMILE, AN ANTHOLOGY

Life is a mosaic of dreams pursued, paths forged, and moments cherished. This anthology brings together the voices of seven remarkable authors—some award-winning, others emerging—to explore the profound question of what it means to live a life that either mirrors our deepest hopes, surpasses them in ways we never imagined, or gracefully strives for the closest replica.

Within these pages, you'll find stories of resilience, quiet submission, reinvention, and triumph. Each contributor offers a unique perspective on the art of crafting a life that feels both authentic and meaningful. From the pursuit of purpose to the beauty of everyday grace, these narratives remind us that life is not just of where we are and what we've learned.

This collection invites you to reflect on the subtle moments that shape the journey ahead.

As you read, may you find inspiration in the shared humanity and kindness that binds us all.

With gratitude.

WITH THE RIGHT ATTITUDE

(YOU CAN DO ANYTHING)

DEL STAECKER

T HEN, IT WAS TERRIBLE BEING middle aged and
divorced. Not a good time. That year I did not
look forward to the holidays. The prospect of again
spending the holidays by myself was depressing. I
plodded forward without much enthusiasm.

On Thanksgiving, I learned my sister died in a
car crash while delivering meals to the homeless.
Five weeks later, on Christmas Eve, I was told that
my mother died. On New Year's, I traveled home
from her funeral to face cancer surgery the next day.

How could things possibly get worse?

But they did.

When discharged from the hospital, I drove
myself home and got the news I had been fired.

Did I mention I was broke, and would soon have no place to live?

Some might say it was my time to sink or swim. But I did not see it that way. Rather than act, or even react, I took time off... Just to think.

Life has its cycles.

It was not my first time at the bottom of a trough, but it was my deepest. I was not happy. I was unemployed, alone, and adrift. I recognized that without major change, I may not rise above this one. I knew that a fresh approach to life was needed, so I committed one hundred percent to altering my condition.

To the friend who gave me a place to stay, I said, "I am going to change everything."

"How?" he asked.

"By focusing on the positive side of life," I replied.

"Mind over matter?" he said, with more than a hint of sarcasm. "It's been tried."

"I know. But I'm going to open myself up only to possibilities based upon goodness," I told him. "Oh yeah," I added, "I'm also going to write a novel."

"Why?"

"Because I always wanted to."

What happened next may sound absurd, but literally within moments of publicly declaring my intent to embrace only the affirmative side of life, I received guidance on what my course should be.

It came in an e-mail from an old friend.

For quite some time my college roommate had been sending me job notices, which I had routinely ignored. He had studied electrical engineering while I had focused on history. The jobs he shared were always technical in nature. I was unsuited for every one of them... Until the last one.

For the first time ever, my old friend shared a job that fit me.

An adventure company was looking for a director of operations—a jack-of-all-trades type, someone knowledgeable in hiking and rafting on one hand, while riding herd over wilderness guides and tending to customers on the other.

Tossed in the mix were a remote Idaho mountain location and just enough money to live on. It was perfect.

I sold everything I had, bought a one-way ticket, and plunged into the opportunity.

I also began to write.

After some months, another friend came to visit me and enjoy rafting on the Salmon River. I showed her my book. She loved it and encouraged me to keep writing.

She also loved me and later that year we were married.

My life indeed was changed by my new attitude.

That was almost two decades ago. I finished my novel, and also several more. All have received wonderful reviews. One has been called a literary masterpiece. Additionally, I penned an historical account of World War Two's most amazing ship which has received several awards.

I, too, have been honored. In 2012, I was selected as a *Writer on Deck* for the U.S. Navy. I have twice been nominated *Author of the Year* by the Military Writers Society of America.

For those skeptical of the power of making a change in life, I can only say, "Try it."

I believe that with the right attitude you can do anything.

ABOUT THE AUTHOR

DEL STAECKER

DEL STAECKER IS AN AWARD-WINNING American writer of novels, novellas, short stories, and non-fiction in a number of genres, including suspense, crime, philosophical fiction, satire, and memoir.

He is a Life Fellow of the Royal Society of Arts (London) and Knight of Honor, Order of St. John (Malta). He was educated at The Citadel, Wheaton College, and The University of Puget Sound.

From Strength to Strength

K. S. Luke

*"I talk to shooting stars
but they always get it wrong,
I feel stupid when I pray.
So why am I praying anyway,
if nobody's listening?" - Demi Lovato*

My PARENTS DID NOT CHOOSE the name, "Grace" for her. Neither as her first nor for her middle, and I can understand that.

In pictures I have seen of her babyhood, she was not so lithe or delicate to have suggested it, and my mother had not yet embraced a life of religiosity that would have steered her in that direction.

They instead settled on Cynthia, or Cindy as we called her. Or, as she would proudly announce to others when she first began speaking and was asked, "Cincy Mame".

It sounded like a precocious attempt to declare her name before she was even able to pronounce or properly vocalize it. It sounded as if she wanted to ensure that it was registered in the minds of those who took the time to look down into her earnest little face and get the gist of her. It seemed like she knew, even at that young age, that she could be a force in life. A name to remember.

This may seem like a very odd comparison, but I once saw a specific photo of Winston Churchill and instantly thought of a picture of my sister when she was a toddler. She looked nothing like the man, of course. She was an attractive child and eventually grew into a beautiful woman in many admirers' eyes, but there was some subtle, unexpected resemblance there.

Maybe it was that mischievous spark in the eyes, a determined look of strength about the jaw and slight tilt of head, or those enigmatic, half-grinning lips that portrayed a sense of wry amusement. It goes without saying that she did not have his ever-present cigar protruding from her mouth, but I could see an equation between the two. He refused to accept weakness and defeat in life, as would she.

I believe she was born with an inner strength very few of us are fortunate enough to possess.

My mother told me a story about Cindy when she was in the 4th grade, or maybe the 5th, and being teased about being larger than her classmates. In her school and family photos from that time, she was slightly taller than the rest of her friends and our cousins of the same age, but not truly overweight. In fact, she looked skinnier than most kids growing up now with more fast food and junk food options than we had access to back in the 1960s and '70s.

In hindsight, it was probably her presence that was bulkier than many of her peers, not her body.

Even now when she appears in my dreams, she towers over everyone in the room, and I can spot her instantly. In real life she was just a few inches taller than me, so that likely stems from my perception of her.

She enlisted my mom's help in shaving off some unhealthy calories, and then she stuck with that business model throughout her lifetime. She was already demonstrating just how purposeful she could be once setting her mind on a task. It seems to me quite rare and impressive for a young child to be so self-directed—to plot a course and find the resolve to stick with the journey. But, I may just be biased.

By the time she entered junior high school, she was already beginning to collect a small stream of satellite-boys who might randomly pass by her in space and then be drawn into her orbit. Our family would stop for the night at a hotel with a pool, for instance, and while I was clumsily splashing around, practicing my swimming skills, there would suddenly be a boy circling her in the deep end like a shark before spending the rest of the evening chatting her up with one arm thrown over the concrete rim of the pool to keep himself afloat.

Or we could be picnicking in a state park a couple of hundred miles from home and look up to see a hopeful suitor straying our way in faded bell-bottom *Levis*, a shaggy haircut, and a triumphant smile after hitchhiking his way towards her even though they had just recently met.

It brings to my mind a sitcom where a brilliant female scientist says, "Come for the breasts, stay for the brains".

While she was in no way considered buxom, most males could instantly recognize those superior frontal lobes in her skull. It was not that she had the fashionable looks or style that would have gained her an instant invitation to sit with the popular girls at the lunch table, or to try out for the cheer-leading squad.

She was more like the heroin in the novel, *Cluny Brown*, whose features may not have been classically beautiful but whose spirit and force shown through clearly enough to let everyone feel as if they were looking at somebody special.

Gravitational force may be the weakest of the four, but it was strong in her being and I believe it derived from her iron core.

It was iron ore that first drew her onto her future life's track and eventually led her down the tunnel into a career as a mining engineer.

After initially landing a job in the offices of *US Steel*, she jumped at the chance when the management asked for volunteers to help with physical labor in other areas. And then she was hooked for the rest of her life on hard-rock mining. She was also beginning to develop a rock-hard body and would eventually compete for years as an amateur on the body building circuit, all the while returning to college to earn her engineering degree, meeting the man who would become her second husband, and continuing to work.

Because her husband was also in the mining industry, she often would have to relocate with him as he was progressing in his career. Most often, they could share a home and both be employed by the same company or in nearby mines, but occasionally she might have to compromise and settle for whatever position was available in a somewhat remote location.

One year she might find herself bartending at a tiny watering hole near the mining man-camps for minimum wage and tips, and the next being hugely compensated at the Yucca Mountain Nuclear Waste Repository without a true sense of direction because of the inherent secrecy and compartmentalization.

There was a stint as a delivery driver for *UPS* and a memorable dark night after taking a wrong turn on a poorly marked lane before *GPS* became available—thinking she was heading toward a ranch house but finding herself instead climbing ever higher up into the hills and gearing down on a two-track dirt road with no way to turn around before embarrassedly pulling up in front of a very confused couple at their solitary tent site.

I would bet they have laughingly told that same story from their viewpoint, as well.

Even before she had received her degree, she was being asked by her professors to help teach other students how to map mines since she excelled at that. Delivery routes, maybe not so much.

Although she had started her engineering education at a slightly older age than a typical student, she had, at that point, been working on and off in various mining positions for years. So, she shot off like a rock star as soon as the bell rang, she was handed her degree, and the doors flew open like grade school at the beginning of summer.

It was not the first, but one of her most memorable positions was that of a production engineer at a mine in Nevada in the process of being closed and reclaimed. It would become the first underground mine in that state's history to receive full closure and reclamation approval. And, it would bring her accolades, since she was instrumental in the process.

It also brought continued job offers from other mines, but she always tried to juggle her career along with her husband's. They would eventually accept positions enabling both parties to equally excel and allow them to purchase property in a somewhat centralized location near the area where his family lived and where she could house her growing menagerie of animals.

While he was commuting on a weekly basis to a gold mine in a neighboring state, she was daily commuting to a silver mine and returning to feed her beloved llamas, their dog Nugget, an assorted flock of adopted chickens, and a few specially ordered Japanese running ducks that, sadly, were unable to outrun the local coyotes.

He held the position as plant manager at his mine, and she would become a chief engineer at hers—and there had been talk of future advances for her as well.

My sister could have easily remained married to her first husband. By all signs he loved her dearly.

But, he had hoped she would eventually settle with him in the sleepy eddies of South Dakota, living a tranquil farming life with family swirling around.

Maybe she would have had children and then grandchildren if she'd stayed on that rural route. And then I could have been a beloved aunt.

Maybe I would still be able to reach her on a land-line now and then to dish about life and pass along a good recipe, talk about her llamas and ducks, my cat and garden.

Maybe she could have always remained older than me.

Maybe someday I'll figure out a more elegant way of talking to shooting stars that does not result in disappointment for me and a discounting of other peoples' wishes, because that is not at all who she was or where she needed to be.

Maybe the stars are not getting it wrong, just me, because she preferred the current.

The long hours of her work and of her workouts to remain competitive in body building, along with the struggles of living somewhat separately from her husband took their toll, and she began suffering from bruxism—clenching and grinding her teeth at night.

Perhaps it was nocturnal anxieties after a day of facing the world with her chin forward. Maybe it was a subconscious need to increase the strength in her jaws, gearing up for a fight and preparing to bite back at any future attackers in life.

I, personally, may have stepped back a little—reassessed, retreated to a corner. But she was not the type to back down. She simply researched, reorganized herself, put her head down and charged full on—butting against all comers like the Aries that she was.

So, a mouth guard was purchased to prevent any damage to her teeth and jaws at night, biofeedback sessions were scheduled, and then she continued taking a bite out of life by day.

You can imagine then, as she was at the height of her career, when she eventually found the words to compose an email informing us of her diagnosis of ALS, the shock completely took my breath away.

Powerless is just another word until you feel it creep into your core.

Horror is, too, before it slams the backs of your knees and punches you in the gut before burrowing deep down into your brain. The realization sinks in, as you collapse in on yourself and down onto the couch, that she will soon be locked into an immovable body with her brilliant mind still intact.

It is like knowing you will be forced to watch as someone is being buried alive in front of your eyes—slowly, oh so slowly, shovelful by shovelful.

Her physicality was so very tightly woven into her being. All those years of building and honing and chiseling her body and her strength, and it was all going to start slipping through her fingers... Literally.

One of the first signs of her muscle failure was as simple as an inability to turn her ignition key— just a slight weakness in her grip. She was hoping it was a pinched nerve, but no such luck.

There was sometimes a stubbing of toe or tripping of foot when it did not rise to meet the occasion of a curb. There was an increasing heaviness in the limbs, an odd muscle twitching here, a slight slurring of words there. By the time she finally steeled herself to email me, she had been to multiple doctors and neurologists hoping to discover a solution.

After a slew of tests they were able to rule out everything that could be causing her symptoms. Everything except ALS—which is the typical experience for most victims.

I can almost picture her middle-of-the-night tossing before each visit to the next specialist, hoping beyond hope it would be something, anything, curable or survivable. It makes me wonder if she still had bruxing issues amid the test anxiety, or if the muscles in her jaws were already weakening too much to produce any more clenching or gnashing of teeth.

I can almost taste that sharp, metallic adrenaline flavor in the mouth as she realized she was in the deep end without the strength to hold onto that concrete rim, where she had so nonchalantly flirted with a young boy in what must have seemed at the time to be an infinity pool.

I am not sure how long it took for her or her husband to get through their initial shock-and-denial stage, or how deep the anger and sense of hopelessness became, or if she had something akin to the 'dark night of the soul' even though she was not religious.

My sister had always enjoyed a glass of good wine at the beach or in the evenings at home. I remember seeing a sign hanging on her kitchen wall, HOW MERLOT CAN YOU GO, which seems somewhat prescient now, because watching someone navigating ALS is like watching them do the limbo dance.

She had set the bar high for herself in life, but now it was being lowered forcefully and rapidly and she would continually need to find ways to gracefully arc backwards and under at every turn just to stay in the game.

Since she could no longer turn the key to her truck, they purchased a remote starter. When she couldn't keep up with chores around the house, they hired help. As she began to weaken more and it was no longer safe for her to go underground in her mine, she brought even more focus into her office. When she struggled to keep up with her protein and caloric intake, her company purchased a microwave so she could easily warm up meals by her desk.

As her gait became progressively more unsteady, a good friend gifted her a special cane fashioned from a bull penis to help raise her spirits and keep her sense of humor intact—even while finding herself in need of a crutch.

When she could no longer lift herself out of her recliner, she purchased one that tilted to help her rise. As she began to lose finger dexterity and could not type as easily, she switched to an *iPad* with a digital stylus and relied more on her secretary.

When it became apparent that her speaking ability was declining, she loaded eye-tracking software onto her computer that could eventually vocalize for her and started practicing. And, when she was no longer able to ride her bike around Lake Coeur d'Alene, she hit the trails in her new neon-green power wheelchair she nicknamed Envy.

Employees of the mine began organizing work crews at her house to lay in cords of firewood in advance of winter, along with other general maintenance—even though she was not the type to have accepted any help before her illness.

I believe she was learning grace out of necessity. She had always been impactful to others, and so when her employers, her coworkers, her friends, her stepchildren, and in-laws who lived near her had to watch her bending further and further to accommodate the limbo stick, they were there to encourage and support.

Not everyone was though, because as her muscles began to fail her, so did her loving and previously supportive husband.

It turns out that not every male stays for the brains, because hers were still fully intact even as her body began to weaken. And when he chose to begin a new life with another woman, my resilient, mining sister starting digging deeper.

Any outsider may have already viewed her as almost played out at that point—with continually fading resources left on which to draw—but she had a proven track record at closing out old chapters and finding imaginative ways to re-contour scarred landscapes.

While I was ineffectually praying for any intervention, she was busy reclaiming her life and her self. She was revising her original blueprint and would many times tell us all, "Do not cry for me."

The final stage of grief, according to some, is that of acceptance and hope. She began to find the former for herself, but the hope that she scraped up was mainly channeled towards future victims of the disease.

She may not have been able to lift weights any longer, but she remained in training mode, educating herself on ways to stay mentally strong through her journey and helping to lift others suffering from the same condition.

She was able to pool resources from her present and former mining companies to raise money for awareness, and funding for her local ALS support group. She helped initiate a benefit ride that raised hundreds of thousands more.

She flew to Washington, D.C. to help advocate for government action, even though she was in a wheelchair at that point.

She used her hard-earned knowledge of nutrition to maintain her strength and quality of life as long as possible, even while her doctors were advising her that she should go with a gastrostomy, since swallowing becomes very difficult for ALS patients. She chose not to go that route and decided instead to create her own meal and protein shake regime higher in healthy fats, proteins, and nutrients than the liquid diet that normally accompanies a stomach feeding tube.

I told her once it was a good thing it worked out well for years, otherwise she would've had to eat crow and that may have been impossible to swallow. She couldn't fully smile, but I got to enjoy again that half-grin and amusement in her eyes.

Ironically, one of her last main battles would be keeping on enough weight to prevent herself from wasting away. Her body, as she said, was in the business of losing muscle and there was never really any hope of recovery from the first diagnosis.

Maybe Joni Mitchell was right when she sang "Something's lost, but something's gained in living every day", because my sister ended up leaving with less, yet somehow more strength and resolve than she possessed when she first arrived in life and that she developed throughout her too brief time here.

It may have morphed from physical to mental strength, but it was just as solid. Maybe not rock solid, but as that weakened exterior began to crack and eventually fall away, an entirely new vein of gold was exposed.

I spotted a stray kitten in the park today as I sat on a creekside bench, chewing on my thoughts and a veggie sandwich, jotting down memories in a college-ruled notebook balanced on my knee. She was lightly damp and caked with mud as if she had been abandoned in last night's thunderstorm or possibly had found herself suddenly washed down the creek bed and needing to claw her way back up the bank to safety.

She was bedraggled and skeleton thin as only cats can be after a dunking, but there was still a spark in her eye, a defiant posture, a loud mew that spoke of determination despite some recent setbacks.

Something makes me believe her look of hope is more about life rather than just a bite of my sandwich.

She reminds me of my sister.

I have decided I will take her home with me.

I think that I shall call her Grace.

ABOUT THE AUTHOR

K. S. LUKE

IMAGE: AUTHOR'S SISTER, CINDY MOORE after a long shift underground.

**Photo reproduced from the *Pioneering the Field: Women in Mining* exhibit at the National Mining Hall of Fame and Museum.

"The submission is a mainly factual account and poignant journey through my sister's accomplishments and struggles in life. It is an example of an individual's ability to empower oneself in the midst of weakness." ~ K. S. Luke

The author currently resides in the red rocks of southern Utah with her husband, three dogs, a wish for a kitten, and the hope that there will soon be a cure for the devastating disease, ALS.

She holds a Bachelor of Science in Integrated Studies with a Biology & Psychology emphasis.

FLEA BITE

CLIFFORD L. CARTER

S HOT OUT OF BED BY the smell of bacon and eggs seeping under my bedroom door, flanked by the sound of Mother's footsteps gliding across scalloped-wool carpet, brushing along a well-worn path. Gliding through a testament of early American pine furniture made by none other then *Ethan Allen*. Buffet on the left, dining table to the right. Stepping closer and closer...

Whack! Whack! Whack!

"Hurry every chance you get," passing Mother's lips like a boot-camp drill sergeant calling to muster a platoon of recruits.

That day I woke myself imagining peanut butter knifed over three pancakes, stacked ever so neatly... Covering the top with warm maple syrup, running down all sides. Next, adorning the tower with two extra thick strips of bacon—burnt to a crisp. A sunny-side-up egg—spearing the yellow until it dribbled down that fluffy tower of delight.

I knew full well what that day would bring. Just like most Saturdays that came before, and all but one or two of the Saturdays that would come after, until I, myself, would hear the voice of a Navy drill sergeant calling me to muster only days after my hair was cut to the scalp... And thank God Mother's training on military creases falling over the bedside tight enough to bounce a quarter had stuck to me like peanut butter to pancakes.

That day may have started out in some ordinary fashion, but how it proceeded would be anything but ordinary.

Jumping into Mother's candy-apple red *Ford Galaxy 500* with two long side doors, opening with a length that pushed my imagination—it was no ordinary automobile. A car that would surely take flight and soar to the galaxy befitting its name.

* * *

Mother's pride and joy... Secured by scraping together every penny, selflessly working at *Saint Joseph's Hospital* in Alton, Illinois, serving lunch to the staff, visitors, as well as making trays for the convalescing patients.

As she toiled over gelatin, mashed potatoes, and Salisbury steak along with her dreams of a new car... I mean, new-to-Mother 'new' car. Not just *any* car, but the one she had her sights set on all the way back to her days working at *Owen Illinois Glass Factory* on East Broadway across from the iconic *Fast Eddie's*.

I remember that place as a small child, because we loved to park in a graveled area along the roadside and watch the little train car up in the sky traveling from one building to another, back and forth, dreaming of the best-ever carnival ride my little mind could comprehend.

When a resident of Wood River, Illinois finally placed an advertisement in the used car section of the *Alton Telegraph* offering a two-door candy-apple-red *Ford Galaxy 500*, black vinyl seats, matching a perfectly topped black vinyl, trimmed with chrome accents, Mother's eyes lit up like a fourth of July sparkler.

She had saved enough and was able to negotiate a modest discount with just enough left over to fill the tank with high octane gasoline from the *Sinclair* station down Fosterburgh Rd, at the curve we called Forkeyville.

"Ma'am, that surely is a beautiful car," the attendant said after mother commanded a fill up.

So proud she was of her new car, "You're not telling me anything I don't already know. I just picked her up for a song and a dance."

Mother paid the man and gave the car a few pumps on the gas before she shifted into drive and spun the tires through a patch of loose gravel in the direction of the gas station attendant who could not keep his eyes off the sparkle of Mother's new car's chrome rear bumper.

She proceeded to rip down the highway, leaving everyone in her rear-view mirror. Smiling with a prideful grin until her favorite green chiffon hair scarf pealed right off the top of a perfectly per-fected tease-up, cemented only by *AquaNet*.

Standing on the breaks from fifty-five MPH to a dead stop in less than thirty seconds, I suppose.

"Get out there and get my scarf," she shouted. "That was a gift from your grandmother."

Wow, I thought to myself. *Those breaks must be red hot by now.*

Back in and down Fosterburgh Road, turning right at Bassette Lane. Another right three doors down and into the drive with the ease of a *PanAm* jet airplane landing at St Louis Missouri's *Lambert Field.*

My task that and every other day was to open the garage door just long enough for Mother to make her entrance. Then down again quick enough so not one passersby could have a look inside her temple we called a garage which held the literal apple of Mother's eye.

* * *

Mother said, "Today, we are going on an adventure. First, *Hill Top Auction* has a Saturday flea market, and then we are heading to that new ceramic shop off Bunker Hill road."

Same as last Saturday, I thought.

"They called and said our greenware was ready for its final glaze before returning to the kiln for one last fire."

Hill Top Auction was an amazing place with all sorts of collectibles. I mostly liked the old beer cans and bottles that were filled with dirt, as if they had just been taken from what they thought had been their final resting place only to be rehabilitated by a garden hose and bottle brush.

I had, most likely, the biggest beer can collection in Madison County. You see, my father built a shelving unit from floor-to-ceiling height and about twenty feet long in the basement out of two-by-fours—just to hold my massive collection.

Almost every time we went coon hunting and came across a dump, I was elbow deep in search of the holy grail. That would be a *Griesedieck Western Stag* cone-top beer can—mint condition of course. If not, I had a trick up my sleeve using *Drano* drainpipe cleaner to dissolve the rust. As long as I caught it in time, the paint would stay in tact.

I knew that because I still have a few nameless cone top beer cans that were left in that caustic solution long enough to de-label.

Rolling into the flea market, searching for a parking spot far away from any driver who might get close enough to ding the door of Mother's spotless shine. I flung open the passenger wing and ran to the tables of treasures inside the main building, barn, lean to, and beaten down by the sun in a heap of fun.

Mother, however, was much more reserved as she glided between tables of knickknacks, discreetly reaching for her holy grail.

That would be a pink *Miss America* butter dish with a dome lid. I can attest she had come across so many that *almost* fit the bill but would fall short with Mother's discerning touch. She would say without a word it was all in the handling.

I watched her choose not any old piece of glass-ware. After making eye contact, her hands would surely decide. Gliding over every piece as if she were in search of some particular marking or authentic dent or wrinkle found that might identify its true nature.

Continuing to walk the route in and out of tables and odd bookshelves flanked by barrel-glass-front china cabinets, she continued her inspection—handling each found object until it either made it to the check stand or was left behind in a pile of *almost* good enoughs.

That day I came across a flat-top *Flagstaff* beer can. I had one already, but that one sported a few less dents and rusty spots than the one that graced my shelves.

I'll sell the old one and make enough to pay for this one, with a few coins to boot.

"Get in the car," Mother said. "I should have already been painting that Christmas tree. We still have to choose a color and put a couple coats of paint on before the final firing. Grandma's been wanting one of those ceramic Christmas trees with the little twinkle lights for years. The lights are supposed to come with the tree and I can tell you I won't spend one red cent more on the glaze or the firing than agreed upon."

I cannot say I was looking so forward to the ceramic shop myself. I'd have rather been out scouting for beer cans.

Although, there is a dump on the side of the road just before the turn off next to a giant oak tree that got hit by lightning a few years ago... We'll see if I can talk Mother into stopping there for a minute or two while I have a look around.

For me, the ceramic shop was like an old lady coffee clutch. Oohing and aahing over each other's attention to detail, color choice, and overall technical skills needed to slop on a coat of paint. Usually all eyes were on the boy with his mother, scraping and cleaning greenware (unfired items), quietly brushing on coats of paint, as Mother chattered away about her favorite pecan pie recipe.

As we rolled into the parking lot, the owner came right out to the car in tears, telling my mother that someone had placed their ceramic Jack O'Lantern too close to Mother's Christmas tree. It had fallen over, creating a very small chip in Mother's project.

"I don't even want to look at it," Mother proclaimed. "I'll start a new tree at your expense, of course, or that clumsy old bat's. I don't really care who pays as long as it's not me, and I get my tree finished in no longer than two more weeks... As it is going to my son's grandmother well before the Christmas holiday."

I was thinking, *This shop owner knows my mother pert' near as good as I do*—in regard to Mother's attention to detail and unwillingness to compromise, as the owner agreed, then invited us into the shop.

Mother never once looked at that damaged tree nor spoke to the woman who caused the kerfuffle in the first place.

I, however, sat down to a perfectly detailed ceramic hound dog with big floppy ears. I knew already it would be painted black and tan—just like my coon-hound pup.

Echo was the greatest gift ever from a close relative. My uncle, Ivan found Echo on the side of the road down in southern Illinois, close to where he lived. He knew full well when he heard Echo's ball-mouth bark, he would be the perfect addition to our coon hunting pack.

Not saying a word while the shop owner offered a ceramic tree that she herself had finished to the point of one last coat of paint, Mother quietly listened until the owner paused, and then Mother exclaimed that she in no way could accept the workmanship of something not quite up to her standard.

Marching back to the inventory of greenware, Mother choose the biggest ceramic Christmas tree that shop owner had and said. "I will take that one. At no charge, of course. Put it on that woman's tab out there and maybe she'll learn a valuable lesson."

Again, the shop owner agreed, removing the large tree from the shelf and placing it on the table for Mother to delicately sand and burnish, readying it for its first fire.

We finished up for the day and said our goodbyes when the phone in the shop rang out. One of the patrons asked mother, "Charlene, are you going to the auction tonight? Harmon's auction house advertised an estate sale in the *Thrifty Nickel* last week."

"Oh? I didn't see that," Mother said. "I'm going right home to fix some dinner and talk my husband into taking me with the truck... In case I find something that won't fit in the back of my new *Galaxy*

500 sitting out there in the parking lot, you see? What time does it start?" Mother asked.

"Six o'clock sharp. That's what the advertisement said anyway. You know Harmon. They're going to start when they are good and ready."

"I'll see you there, Judy." Mother turned to me. "Now, let's hurry up and get down the road."

We took off, forgetting I had asked to stop at the roadside dump.

I'm not saying a word. I figured it was useless. When mother had her mind set on an auction, there was no chance of getting in the way.

The only thing more exciting than a flea market was *Harmon Estate Auction.* Mother had filled the house with collectibles, proclaiming they would some day be her retirement. I knew better that she would more likely be buried with her treasures than let anyone else get even one good look at her stash.

I also knew it would be hot dogs and *Chef Boyardee* chili for dinner, because it takes time to freshen up hair and makeup and, of course, choose a new outfit. 'Lord knows we can't have that woman at the ceramic shop seeing us in the same old rags twice in one day.' As powder puffed and patted Mother's face, I imagined her perfecting an emotionless poker face, so she was sure to outbid, or at the very least out intimidate, any other potential buyer she came across.

I wondered for a long time why my mother always sat so close to the passenger door when Dad was driving his old hunting truck. Maybe she was afraid.

Sitting between him and her was a spit-filled *Tab* soda can filled with masticated *Red Man* chewing tobacco.

Well, it had nothing to do with that and everything to do with who gets out before other auction goers with time enough to rummage through the rows and rows of tables, in and out of boxed goods searching for a treasure.

"Sit down. It's about to start. Your father is most likely outside with a cup of coffee and a fried cherry pie shooting the breeze with his hunting buddies about your dog, Echo."

You could count on the auctioneer to give a pretty good description of what was up for sale at the time bidding started, as well as lifting the energy level in the room—likened to a feeding frenzy of hungry piranha.

"Hey, bidder. Hey, bidder. Give me one dollar. Now, give me two dollar. Now, give me three."

That went on until everyone had stopped bidding. Then the last and highest bidder was awarded the item. Along the way, the auctioneer was, what I would say, 'talking crap' about an item he most likely had little to no idea of its value, origin, markings or anything else.

One thing you could take to the bank was you'd see the auctioneer's helper running their hands all over a piece of ceramic or depression glass. That might have been where Mother adopted said ritual. A time or two, the auctioneer would confess there may have been a little chip on the edge of a beautiful piece of glassware.

"Hey, bidder. Hey, bidder. We got a nice little *Miss America* butter dish. Looks to be in perfect condition accept for a flea bite just on the bottom edge."

At the start of commentary, I noticed Mother's breathing increase as her adrenaline began rising and rising, holding her bidding arm down until the auctioneer finished and started with the business of deciding last offer in the room.

When he got to the flea bite, Mother's face looked as if she'd seen a ghost and her bidding arm fell to the seat in such a failing that yet another obsession ended in disappointing imperfection.

The story of antique acquisition through yard sale, auction, flea market, or family heirloom was simply a metaphor depiction Mother's dependence on perfection. The idea a treasure might make it into our home would always be of first-class quality fit and finish of whatever was needed or wanted by Mother's adorning eye.

This translated to people as well as inanimate objects.

I can remember on more than one occasion cruising down the highway and hearing Barbara Streisand's beautiful and very perfect voice coming over the car radio. It would last only a minute before the channel was changed to some less assuming melody.

I asked Mother once why she didn't like the sound of Barbara Streisand and she said, "When I hear her voice, all I can think about is her big nose."

I imagine it was not at all much different than peering at a flea-bit piece of pink *Miss America*.

Those judgments had no bounds, as displayed so boldly at the annual family reunion held outside in the summer sun at *Winchester Western Club* grounds.

Piling out of Mother's *Galaxy 500,* walking not too close behind aunt Nancy, I heard a whispering in my ear.

"Looks like two *Volkswagen Beetles* trying to pass each other," Mother said.

Nancy was a large woman, to be honest, but did Charlene need to point it out in such a visually disturbing way?

Years later, after I came back from the service, I started working and became desperate to leave home. I found a small studio apartment in Wood River that had been converted from a garage into an almost livable space.

It was not so bad, really, especially after I hung a life-size poster of James Dean (my young adult crush) on the only door leading to a dusty furnace and water heater. I'm certain Mother and Dad thought it was a total waste of the little money I earned working at the *Alton Square Mall.* I was the assistant manager, and later store manager, at the *Chess King* in men's fashion clothing—matching a top to pant, sock to shoes, and so on and so forth.

I really wanted a television for my new digs, not to pass the time but so it might drown out the family of skunks living under the garage's floorboards.

Most every night, I'd hear the awfullest sounds of fighting—like two cat gangs scrapping over turf. I knew it was not cats because the smell that followed was all to memorialized by stink that permitted the floor, walls, clothing, and just about anything that would hold on to it—including me.

Once I got to the mall, my first stop was the *Macy's* men's cologne counter for a few sprays of camouflage.

I knew in Mother's frequent *Hill Top Auction*, *Harmon's*, and numerous flea markets and antique shops excursions she was bound to run across a too-cheap-to-pass-up television set to drown out the skunk wars under my place of residence.

Sure enough, one evening my mother and father stopped by with a garage-warming gift. As my father backed up the truck, I hurriedly ripped down the James Dean poster he clearly had already seen in the side mirror since the front door was wide open with a clear shot to the furnace room door.

Once Dad dropped the tailgate, I set my eyes upon what appeared to be a rose-gold-colored tea cart with clear plastic roller feet and two *Formica* shelves.

"Picked up a T. V. and stereo, including a cart at *Hill Top Auction* last Monday," Mother said.

Dad and I unloaded the TV, eight-track tape player and stereo, two speakers the size of a full loaf of bread, and a set of rabbit ears that reached practically from floor to ceiling.

"We don't have time to set it up but I'm sure you can figure that part out," Mother quipped as they hurried back to the truck. They sped off only after she rolled down the window to say, "Hope you like it."

James went right back up on that door before I even thought about setting up this almost-good-enough piece of history.

I remember about ten years earlier I had asked for a cassette stereo for Christmas, and only after consulting with my older brother—who informed them they should get me an eight-track tape player instead. I'm sure it was because he had a box full of eight-track tapes he wanted to listen to on my stereo. Nonetheless, that Christmas as I hoped for the latest version of Hi-Fi, I was disappointed to see an eight-track tape player neatly wrapped with a big Santa smile, as if Santa knew I would be let down the moment I tore through his fluffy white beard.

That night, James and I made popcorn, hooked up the TV and stereo, faced those rabbit ears toward the ceiling, got a pillow from my makeshift bed/sofa, and turned my parent's most generous gift on.

First off, I noticed a flash in the middle of the screen that got bigger and bigger as it moved in all directions, simultaneously filling the glass. Then, what we use to call 'snow' appeared, along with what we would describe today as 'white noise' coming from the speaker. I moved the rabbit ears every direction possible and then resorted to crinkling up and entire box of aluminum foil to extend the reach in order to capture a signal.

I did get a glimpse of Andy Griffith when I squinted and moved my head up and down fast enough to still the image that continually rolled from top to bottom like a bingo cage housing hundreds of letter balls.

After about an hour of fumbling around with the TV, I turned on the stereo. White noise flooded those speakers pretty much the same as what came out of the television set.

Not sure in the end if that was better than 'Skunk Wars' but the white noise did help me sleep—as long as I kept the covers over my head so that offensive smell wouldn't keep me up all night.

I waited a few days before I called Mother to inform her about the television that she and Father so kindly and thoughtfully bought for me. I had a feeling what she would say, because it would likely be the same response when I asked for *Levis* and inevitably got *J. C. Penney's* plain pocket pants to wear to school, giving my fellow classmates yet another reason to push me down into the first mud hole we came across.

When I did call her and thank her for thinking of me, I informed her not that the television was a piece of crap but instead I shared it was a black and white TV and color TVs had been out even before eight-track tape players were replaced by cassettes.

She said, "You are still holding onto the eight -track tape player your brother talked us into buying for you Christmas. Well, he had nothing to do with this or the *J.C. Penney* plain pockets you hated so much.

"My mother and grandmother told me the same thing that I will tell you. Life does not always give you what you want. In fact, most of the time if we can get even close to what we want then we should be happy. I believe somewhere along the way I was told my dime-store Sunday dress had been a *reasonable facsimile* of the cute *Macy's* look-alike shown in the window glass along the sidewalk downtown.

"I guess I adopted the saying and use it every time I get almost what I want. And every time I have given almost what had been wanted. Use this as a life lesson to be thankful for everything and consider yourself to be stronger and wiser for it."

Yes, Mother. If I heard that once, I've heard it a thousand times—coming from your mouth to my ears.

Today, those two words seem to have stuck to me like peanut butter on pancakes. Without even thinking and in need of a wedding ring, my first, second, and third stops were to the local pawn shops for yet another *Reasonable Facsimile*.

ABOUT THE AUTHOR

CLIFFORD L. CARTER

CLIFFORD CARTER HAS ALWAYS BEEN a writer, if only by dreaming of the day he would actualize one single thought placed on a page to be reviewed and marveled at—ever evolving into a style driven by his intuitive nature exploring the world.

Writing has been a way for Clifford to express his feelings onto the page, as they flow in and out of his consciousness, like a river winding through a deep canyon—eventually reaching the sea. With every rock outcropping, another twist and turn surfaces from the dark murky waters of life experience.

Clifford's family, and growing up in a tiny mid-western town, offered a box or vessel-like container that enabled him to turn inward to the safety of his own thoughts. It took a literal tricennial to accomplish his first piece, which became an award-winning mindfulness curriculum followed by a meditation manual.

Charting New Journeys

Mark Fleisher

W ES HODGES ENJOYED A CHALLENGE.

A five-foot-eight-inch, 140-pound sopho-more wouldn't stand much of a chance of making the football team—especially at a high school loaded with college prospects and accurately called a perennial Ohio power.

"Look, son. This isn't pee-wee football," Glendale's assistant coach, Andy DiNardo told him. "I don't mean to hurt your feelings, but you're too small. I don't want to see you get hurt. I appreci-ate you trying. Maybe if you grew a few inches and bulked up some…"

Wes took the advice to heart. Over the next year he hit the gym three or four times a week, adjusted his diet, and the following August when football practice began, he was six-foot and a solid 200 pounds.

"Well, look at you," DiNardo said. "Nice going. Now, let's see what you've got."

Wes worked at third-team safety and linebacker and felt he'd shown enough to make the team. Nothing was official until the coaches announced the first game roster, though.

Wes made the team. His uniform number: 31.

During the regular season, Wes was on the field mostly during garbage time when the Tigers were way ahead and the starters got a breather. He was credited with six tackles, one pass defended, and an interception erased when he caught the ball barely out of bounds. He warmed the bench during the Tigers' state championship win—their third title in six years.

Wes looked forward to his senior year. His grades were excellent. He hoped for more playing time and started thinking about college. Counselors told Wes he more than likely could get into most schools.

One with a football team, he told himself.

That summer Wes met a girl at the gym. Lorrie Farmer was a year behind him, but he knew her name from the stories she wrote in the school newspaper. Lorrie was smart with a great sense of humor. Blonde hair in a pony tail, trim figure and perfect facial features created a beautiful picture.

Steamy August weather meant football practice. Wes had no idea what his role might be.

Would he be relegated to the third team again? Did he have a shot at starting? *Do your best*, he told himself. *And let the chips fall where they may.*

When summer practice ended and the season began in early September, Wes found himself a second-team linebacker and on the punt team. The latter would give him more opportunities to be on the field. The strong Tiger defense would force opponents to punt several times during games.

The Tigers breezed to five straight wins with a winning margin of almost twenty points a game. Wes played some at linebacker, making five tackles. He forced one fumble on the punt team and recovered another that led to a touchdown.

Football cut into his time with Lorrie. They liked each other. As to love, Wes was unsure. He wondered if Lorrie even considered the possibility.

Three days before game six, Wes and Lorrie were eating lunch at a table outside the cafeteria. Mid-October in Ohio, the air fresh and cool, leaves a myriad of colors on the nearby hillsides.

Wes looked up to see Ron Antonovich approaching. Antonovich thought he was the class tough guy. In other words, a bully.

"Hey, Wesley, I see you're still going out with Lorrie Farmer," he bellowed.

"It's Wes, not Wesley. And me going out with Lorrie is none of your damn business."

"Okay, Wesley. By the way hear any good farmer's daughter jokes lately?"

With that, Wes rose from the table, took a step forward and slammed his right fist into his tormentor's mouth.

Antonovich fell backward, breaking his fall by grabbing the side of the table.

Didn't take long for a teacher to step between the two. It was coach DiNardo,

"Sit the hell down, Wes. I don't know what started this, but I have an idea. Doesn't matter. We need to see the boss. Now!"

The boss was school principal, Arnie Fredericksen, formally Doctor Fredericksen, because he had earned a doctor of philosophy degree. His philosophy was simple: Thou shalt not cause any trouble in my school.

"How's Antonovich?" he asked DiNardo.

"One of the other teachers took him to the nurse's office. Looked like he had a split lip and lost two teeth."

Fredericksen was judge and jury. There was no Court of Appeals. Wes related his side of the story, defending Lorrie's honor and giving a bully what he deserved.

"Okay," Fredericksen began. "I applaud your chivalry, Mr. Hodges. And what's-his-name is a bully among other things. But clipping him on the jaw—an overreaction, shall we say, and punishment is in order. You're suspended for a week starting tomorrow morning.

"Obviously you won't be playing football Saturday. As far as the rest of the season is concerned, I'll leave that up to the coaches. You're not to be on campus at all for the week, and you're not to show up at Saturday's game. Understood?"

"Yes, sir. I understand."

"And two other things," the principal continued. "I'll be calling your parents this evening. There's also the possibility that Antonovich's family will press charges against you. I'm sure your parents can expect medical bills from them."

As promised, Fredericksen called Wes's parents that evening. His words were not a total shock as their son had related what he had done and the punishment that followed.

"I don't know this other kid," Ray Hodges told Wes, "but what he did was clearly out of bounds. Considering how you reacted, I think suspending you for a week is fair. As far as your mother and I are concerned, you're grounded for the week as well. In other words, you are restricted to the house."

Antonovich's parents did not press charges. *Maybe they know their son is a real jerk*, Wes thought. They did, however, send Ray Hodges a bill for several hundred dollars of dental work.

"I'll pay it back," Wes told his father. "It might take a while, but I will."

"We'll just add it to your tab," Ray replied. "What about football? Will they let you play?"

"Don't know, Dad. I guess I'll find out next week."

When Wes returned to school the following Thursday, his friends treated him as a conquering hero—pats on the back, high fives and comments that Antonovich deserved what he got.

"Proud of you, Bro," said Elijah Washington, a football co-captain and hulking defensive tackle who was a lock for a Division I scholarship. "I don't know what he's gonna tell you, but I saw coach. He wants you in his office after classes."

While Wes pondered his football future, he also thought about Lorrie. Although they talked and texted, the pair hadn't seen each other during his suspension.

He met her in the hallway between English and history classes.

"I missed you," Wes said.

"Can't talk now," Lorrie said. "I'm late for class. We'll talk at lunch, okay."

The words "we'll talk" sound ominous, Wes thought.

Lunch came after history class, where Mr. Moses welcomed back "Glendale High's newly-crowned heavyweight champ."

Wes saw Lorrie at a table in the back of the cafeteria. He sat down, began to unwrap his lunch—a corned beef sandwich on rye, slathered with mustard, topped with sauerkraut. Two pickles on the side. His Jewish mother made sure Wes appreciated her favorite foods.

"I have a feeling I'm getting the 'I like you but' speech," Wes said.

"No," Lorrie said. "We're moving to California."

"What? Really?"

"My dad's company promoted him to vice-president and he'll be—we'll be—transferring to corporate headquarters near San Francisco. It's a great opportunity for him. We really like Glendale, but there's no way he could pass this up."

"You'll be finishing the school year here, right?" Wes asked.

"Afraid not. Dad's going out there the first week of December and Mom, my brother, and I leave here right after Christmas break. I guess this comes as a shock."

"You're not kidding."

Lorrie put her hand atop Wes's arm. "Um, we could stay in touch and all that. Long-distance relationships... I don't know. I've heard too many stories. Most of them don't work out. I like you, and I want us to be friends no matter where we are."

"Friends? Sure, what the hell. Look, I've got a class in five minutes, and then I need to see Coach Tolliver. Send me a picture of the Golden Gate Bridge, damn it."

With that Wes went off to Spanish class which he sat through immersed in an alternate universe. He could see his classmates and Mrs. Saiz. Whatever they said washed over him. Wes finally returned to the current dimension and headed for the football office.

Coach Tolliver was in his sixth year leading the Tigers football team. He played linebacker at the University of Michigan, serving as a co-captain his senior year when he made all-conference. The New York *Giants* drafted him in the third round. He played four seasons in New York before twice blowing out his right knee ending his career.

He returned to school, got a master's in phys ed, a second master's in English, and took education courses to earn his teacher certification. Tolliver landed a teaching position at a small rural Ohio school and doubled as assistant football coach.

Six years later, the Glendale job opened up. Tolliver was one of a dozen applicants. He got the job.

Despite his academic credentials, Tolliver could come across as a drill instructor. His speech on the first day of practice his first year was legendary. He gathered the team at midfield and according to one participant spoke loud and clear.

"My name is Bennett Lawrence Tolliver. B. L. T. Let me assure you I am not a breakfast or lunch sandwich. I am your football coach. You will address me as Coach, not Mr. Tolliver, not sir, not Ben. Ben is reserved for my family and my friends. You are not my friends. You may wind up not liking me at all. Why? We are going to work hard, very hard. Some of you may decide to quit. Our goal is to develop a team that won't back down, plays hard, and respects each other. When we achieve these goals, we will be a family. And family members love each other, sacrifice for each other, and work together. If there are no questions, let's get going."

Wes knocked on Coach Tolliver's partially open office door.

"Come on in," Tolliver said, as he beckoned Wes to sit. "I think you know the powers-that-be have left it up to me whether to let you back on the team. I know you haven't played that much. But you've done a decent job when you've been on the field.

Dr. Fredericksen told me you're a good student and this is the first trouble you've been in.

"Tell me about yourself. What about college? What about football?"

Wes sat silent for a few moments, trying to collect his thoughts to answer questions he did not expect.

"You know, coach, I like challenges. I'm realistic, though. Man, on our team we've probably got a half dozen four- and five-star recruits. They'll play big-time college football. Me, I'm a one-star recruit at best. But, I'd like to play football at the next level. Maybe I could cut it at Division II. I'd be happy even being a walk-on."

Coach Tolliver leaned back in his chair. "You know, Wes, at some point we're done with x's and o's. I don't think my responsibility ends with coaching football. I like to believe I can help you guys figure out the world beyond high school, beyond football. Any thoughts?"

Boy, Coach Tolliver has really mellowed, Wes thought to himself.

"I know I've got to start thinking about college. I think I'd like to major in history. But what do you do with a history degree? Wind up teaching, I guess? And I don't know if I want to do that."

Coach Tolliver looked at his watch, shook his head, and said he didn't want to hold up Wes any longer.

"It's getting late, and you need to get home. So as far as football is concerned, you're back on the team. You've missed practices so you won't suit up Saturday. But come to practice Monday and we'll move on. And no more incidents. Stay away from Antonovich."

"Thanks, coach. And trust me, I will. I won't let you down."

* * *

Wes opened the back door, walked up three steps into the kitchen where Rebecca Hodges prepared dinner.

"How did school go, sweetheart?"

"Okay, I guess," Wes mumbled. "I'm back on the football team beginning Monday."

"Well, you don't seem very happy about it. Sit down and tell me."

"Coach was great. He was easy to talk to you. I think he's mellowed, Mom. We talked some about football and life."

Rebecca joined Wes at the small table that served as a staging area for her dinner preparations.

"Mellowed? Getting married and having a baby will do that to a man. So, what about life?"

"I don't know," Wes said. "I know I'm not gonna play football at a big school, and he wanted to know if I had any plans down the road—like after high school and college. I said I'd like to play football at a smaller school. The one thing I do know is I'll never be big enough or good enough to play pro football. Other than that, I don't know."

"So maybe you should start thinking about what you want to do in life. I don't think you're interested in your dad's printing business."

"Mom, that's four, five years away. Plans can change. Things can change. Like things with..."

"With what?" Rebecca asked. "Or maybe I should say who. You haven't said a word about Lorrie. Did you see her, talk to her?"

"Yeah, I saw her."

"And?"

"And..."

Before Wes could continue, Ray Hodges came into the kitchen after taking the back door route.

Ray's commercial printing business was booming, often requiring Ray and his employees to put in more than the usual number of hours.

"Long day, but we finished three jobs on schedule," he said. "I thought about going to the gym afterward. No way. Too darn tired. Oh, I saw Larry Brinkman during lunch and he told me the Farmers are moving to California."

"What?" Rebecca said, turning to Wes.

"I was about to tell you when Dad came in. Lorrie's father is leaving in early December and the rest of the family after Christmas break. Nothing more to say."

"Oops. Me and my big mouth," Ray said. "At least you'll have some time to spend with her."

"What's the point, Dad? She'll be two thousand miles away, and I'll probably never see her again. Besides, I'm back on the football team starting Monday, and that's gonna take up most of my time."

The usual lively dinner conversation was subdued as the family enjoyed Rebecca's baked chicken, roasted asparagus, and the ever-present beets—which she claimed aided one's digestive system.

Although he didn't suit up for Saturday's game, Wes joined his teammates on the sidelines. Glendale led throughout but held only a four-point lead late in the final quarter.

The Tigers' opponent, the East Fremont Hawks, had a losing record, but their players were revved up and wanted nothing more than to upset Glendale. With two minutes left in the game, East Fremont faced a fourth down and two yards to go for a first down at Glendale's thirty-seven-yard line.

East Fremont's coaches faced a decision. If a long field try was successful, they'd still be down a point with time running out. If they made the first down, they'd have enough time left to score the winning touchdown.

Their kicker stayed on the sideline, and when the Hawks broke the huddle they lined up in shotgun formation with the quarterback and running back five yards behind the line of scrimmage. The quarterback took the snap, faked to his running back, and hiding the ball on his right hip, headed to his right. A classic bootleg play.

But Glendale's all-state linebacker, Randy Slater smelled the play from its outset. He shed one blocker, then delivered a crushing tackle, resulting in a three-yard loss.

Glendale's fans went wild. Players on the bench high fived and fist bumped. The Tigers had the ball and could run out the clock for their ninth consecutive victory.

But the cheers became an eerie silence when Slater came off the field, right arm dangling at his side, left hand clutching his shoulder. Two trainers escorted Slater to a seat on the bench where they were joined by team doctor, Nate Stokes, and Coach Tolliver.

"We'll put his arm in a sling," Stokes said, turning to Slater. "I don't think it's broken, maybe dislocated, maybe the muscle torn from the bone. We'll take an MRI tomorrow and go from there."

* * *

After classes Monday, Wes hurried to the football complex, changed into his uniform, and headed to the field. The upcoming game was the tenth and last of the regular season before playoffs started.

Randy Slater stood on the sideline talking with Coach Tolliver. They motioned Wes to join them.

"I'm doing okay," Randy said in response to Wes's question. "Still hurts. At least the shoulder isn't broken. Doc Stokes was right. Dislocated and a muscle tear. Won't be able to suit up for the playoffs. Heck, I wish I was the bionic man."

Coach Tolliver looked Wes straight in the eye. "The job is yours, Hodges. I wouldn't say that if I thought you couldn't handle it."

Wes took a deep breath. "Well, coach. I'm not Randy Slater, but I'll do my best out there Saturday."

He did fine Saturday as the Tigers completed an unbeaten regular season with a 27-7 win over the Paxton Pirates. Wes made six tackles—two for losses—batted away two short passes and was credited with a sack of the Paxton quarterback.

The post-game locker room was joyful but not raucous.

"Pretty good job tonight," Coach Tolliver told the team. "A little sloppy here and there. We'll clean that up and get ready for next week."

The following week—the first playoff game—matched the Tigers against the Trent Bulldogs. The experts predicted a tight game. Somebody forgot to tell Glendale, who came away with a 35-6 triumph.

Wes and much of the first-team defense sat out most of the fourth quarter as the coaches wanted to give backups some playing time. He had a solid performance—six tackles, a pass defensed, and two hits on the quarterback. Not arrogant or cocky, but Wes felt his self-confidence rising.

The next several days were like a whirlwind. Coaches had prepared the game plan for their Saturday opponent, the unbeaten Lawrenceville Bombers. Practices were intense, with Glendale players learning new offensive and defensive wrinkles Coach Tolliver and his staff had devised.

Glendale's entourage boarded buses late Friday afternoon for the three-hour trip to Lawrenceville in the southwestern corner of the state. When they arrived and assembled in their hotel, Coach Tolliver had a few words to say.

"We all know how important this game is. Lawrenceville is a tough team, but I think we've prepared very well this week. Next week, I expect we'll be playing for the state championship. What do you guys say?"

A collective "yes" sprinkled with a few "hell, yes"es rose up from the Tigers.

"Okay," Coach Tolliver continued. "After dinner you'll have about two hours free. Bed check at ten. Breakfast at eight in the morning. Then we'll have a brief meeting and head for the stadium. Kickoff at one."

The self-proclaimed experts predicted a tight defensive struggle. They were correct. The score stood 0-0 midway in the second quarter.

"It's gonna be decided on turnovers," Coach Tolliver told his staff. Whoever gets the big break."

And the big break—at least the first one—fell to Glendale when Elijah Washington burst through the Lawrenceville line, sacked the quarterback whose fumble was recovered by defensive back Tre Williams on the Bombers' eleven-yard line.

Two plays later, running back, Ronnie Page scooted around left end into the end zone. The extra point try was good and the Tigers led 7-0 lead at halftime.

Wes and his defensive teammates were rock solid in the second half, keeping Larenceville score-less. Glendale added a late score and now was one victory away from the state title. Wes had a solid game—five solo tackles, three assisted tackles, and one pass breakup.

After a brief locker room celebration, the Tigers returned to Glendale awaiting a week of practice before the following Saturday's state title game.

Their opponent: The Manchester Monarchs.

Coach Tolliver called the practices "crisp". From the starters through the roster everyone had their eye on the prize.

Wes internally admitted to a case of the jitters. *It'll be gone when I make contact with a Monarch,* he told himself.

And on the third play of the game, Wes shed a blocker and solidly tackled a Monarch running back for a two-yard loss.

The teams traded first-half touchdowns. Manchester drew first blood, scoring on a forty-five-yard pass to Rick Richards, their all-state tight end.

T.J. Evans put Glendale on the board with a twenty-three-yard scamper and then hit wide receiver Alex Carpenter with a twenty-eight-yard strike.

The pattern continued into the third quarter. Manchester drew even with another touchdown pass to Richards. Glendale managed a long drive but Manchester held its ground and the Tigers settled for a thirty-yard field goal by Pete Castiglione. He added a twenty-nine yarder in the fourth quarter, giving Glendale a 20-14 lead with three minutes remaining.

Manchester began its potentially game-winning drive on the thirty-three following the kickoff. Three running plays gained seventeen yards but ate up a minute five seconds before the Monarchs took their first of three timeouts.

During the timeout, Elijah Washington gathered the defense. "We all know what we gotta do, guys. Can't let them score. Can't let them score."

Washington looked at Wes and nodded his head, urging him to speak.

"We've worked hard for this moment and I'll tell you I'm not gonna let this slip away from us."

A short Manchester pass gained only three yards, forcing the Monarchs to spend their second time-out. Two more plays gained ten yards, giving the Monarchs a first down but forcing another timeout with a mere twelve seconds left on the clock.

No doubt, the last play would be a desperation pass. Manchester's quarterback took the snap, tight end Richards blocked a Tiger lineman, then drifted into the flat before turning up field.

Wes ran with him, step for step. Richards was three inches taller and twenty pounds heavier. When they reached the end zone, both players soared into the air.

Time seemed suspended.

Richards seemed in position for the catch when Wes extended his right hand and flicked the ball away, ending Manchester's chances and the game.

The Tigers were state champs.

They piled atop each other in celebration. Finally unpiling at midfield, Washington and center Ahmed Robinson hoisted Coach Tolliver on their shoulders. When they released him, T.J. Evans administered the Gatorade bath.

Once in the locker room, Coach Tolliver managed to dry his face and hair with a towel.

"Okay, everybody, gather around. I want you all to know how proud I am of you. When I say all, I mean the players, the coaches, trainers, the student managers... Everybody."

Coach Tolliver reached behind him and held three footballs in his hands. They were already marked with the date and score of the title game.

"Usually one game ball is awarded," he said. "Well, I'm gonna break that tradition and award three. I want to recognize the offensive line. We only had three negative plays all night—and that's nothing short of unbelievable.

"Ahmed, you're the leader of that group, so I'm presenting this game ball to you."

Cheers bounced off the metal lockers and concrete walls. Coach Tolliver called for quiet.

"We all know what kind of player he is. We all know what kind of person he is. He's been the heart and soul of this team for the last two seasons. Despite suffering a nasty injury that ended his season, he attended every practice, stood on the sidelines at every game encouraging you guys, giving you advice along the way. He was like another coach on the field.

"Randy Slater, get your butt up here."

Cheers turned to "Ran-dee, Ran-dee, Ran-dee before Slater held up his hand. "I don't know what to say except, thank you, and I'll remember this moment for the rest of my life. What an honor."

"The last game ball goes to someone who stepped into a difficult situation. He hadn't played very much and some of us wondered if he could step into Randy Slater's shoes."

Holy mackerel, Wes thought. *He's talking about me.*

"Wes Hodges, be proud of what you've accomplished. You deserve this game ball for what you've done these last four games—and all your hard work and effort these last two years."

"Speech, speech, speech," Wes's teammates exhorted.

"All I can say is, I'm honored and thankful you all had faith in me. I love you guys."

"Before everyone gets showered and changed I want to say a few things more," Coach Tolliver said. "We are the Glendale Tigers. We have a tradition to uphold on and off the field. So remember that when you're out there celebrating tonight."

After everyone cleared out, Wes finally changed into street clothes. Sitting on a bench opposite his locker, he cradled the game ball close to his chest and tried to assemble his thoughts.

A voice broke the silence. "Hey, Wes, your mom and dad are outside. You okay?" It was assistant coach, Andy DiNardo.

"Yeah, coach. I'm okay. Just thinking about all that's happened to me these last couple of years. Honestly, I never thought I'd be on a championship team and getting a game ball, too. It's kind of a dream."

"Two years ago I said you were too small to have a chance at making the team. You could have gone home and thrown in the towel. You could have just plain quit. But you didn't. You worked your butt off and here you are. You sure as hell are a resilient son-of-gun, Hodges.

"Now get the hell out of here and go celebrate!"

EPILOGUE

Ray Hodges sold his printing business and he and Rebecca moved to Asheville, North Carolina, an area they had frequently visited and enjoyed.

Randy Slater recovered from his shoulder injury, played four years of football at a major school and was named an All-American his senior season. He was drafted into the National Football League and is in his eighth season. He was named All-Pro three years and proudly wears a Super Bowl ring.

Coach Tolliver led Glendale to two more state titles before retiring. He now writes children's books and lives in Oregon with his wife and two children. His successor: Andy DiNardo.

Dr. Arnie Frederickson died of a heart attack while playing tennis. The school board voted unanimously to name the high school in his memory.

Ron Antonovich got involved in a "chop shop" operation, cannibalizing parts from stolen cars. He is serving a twelve-year sentence in state prison.

Wes Hodges graduated from a small liberal arts college in Minnesota where he played football and made second team all-conference his final year. He received a degree from a prestigious East Coast law school and joined a mid-sized Maryland firm specializing in corporate law. He married an artist, eventually left the practice of law, moved to upstate New York with his wife and two children, and bought a boutique winery.

Wes and Randy Slater remained good friends. Each was the best man at the other's wedding.

Lorrie Farmer remained in California where she earned a degree in journalism and a master's in business administration. Married and divorced, she is vice-president for communications at an international high-tech company.

She never did send Wes Hodges a picture of the Golden Gate Bridge.

About the Author

Mark Fleisher

Mark Fleisher has published six books of poetry and prose. His recent book—*Persons of Interest*—contains a Baker's Dozen of poems and stories.

His fifth book—*Knowing When*—was awarded a 2024 bronze medal for poetry by the Military Writers Society of America (MWSA).

Fleisher, an Ohio University journalism graduate, served in the United States Air Force. He spent a year in Vietnam as an Air Force combat news reporter and received a Bronze Star.

Following military service, he held reporting and editing positions at newspapers in New York State and Washington, D.C.

He is a member of MWSA, SouthWest Writers, and the Albuquerque VA Creative Writing Group.

SANDY REALLY

(A MODERN-DAY CINDERELLA STORY)

SANDRA MILLER LINHART

NOT YESTERDAY...

But a while ago...

There was a plain, ordinary little girl. Her reddish-blond hair played wildly upon her head, making it impossible to tame. Freckles sprayed her cheeks and nose like paint.

An unremarkable girl in all respects. And her name was Sandy Really.

Sandy Really lived on the outskirts of a small rundown town in an adequate but small rundown house in the middle of a small rundown field. In fact, everything about the Wyoming town was rundown—the pool, the school, the store. Everything.

Sandy Really's mother did her best to make their rundown house a comfortable home. She sewed curtains from bright purple, green, and pink material.

She taught Sandy Really how to sew, and together they mended and brightened up the place.

Mrs. Really also cooked the most wonderful treats and meals. She soon taught Sandy to cook, too, telling her someday, somewhere, Sandy Really would make a good *Partner in Life*.

Sandy Really learned to scrub and clean the run-down house into a shiny rundown home.

She planted beautiful flowers and bushes to cover the cracks in the sidewalks and walls outside their home.

She painted stems over the cracks on the walls inside and painted beautiful flowers to match the brilliant curtains.

Sandy Really knew what made things beautiful, and she spent her days growing up practicing her art.

There was nothing Sandy Really couldn't do. Like her mom, Sandy Really could build and paint. She could mend and sew. She knitted. She washed. She planted and gardened and cooked what she grew into tasty treats. The Really's home glowed with love.

One day not long ago...

But not yesterday...

Mrs. Really told her daughter to leave their home to find a *Partner in Life*. She said the best place to find a partner to love and respect you for who you are was in college.

So, at the age of seventeen, like most girls, Sandy Really scolded her hair with a brush, covered her freckles with light brown face paste, and headed off to college.

She drank in the knowledge of books and listened carefully to men and women in long robes who spoke of things she'd never even imagined.

She didn't look hard for a *Partner in Life*, but every time she talked to her mother, she heard how important it was to find the perfect one.

Right before she left the college with a diploma, Sandy Really realized she had failed her mother. She had book knowledge, but not a *Partner in Life*.

She knew she didn't have much time. School would soon be finished, and everyone would be going home. She'd go back to her small rundown house in the middle of a small rundown field on the outskirts of the small rundown town in Wyoming, where finding a *Partner in Life* would be next to impossible.

Sandy Really took her head from her books and looked around.

People surrounded her.

They were learning.

They laughed and talked.

They shared ideas—like the men and women in long robes who taught her. She joined in and soon found herself in a group of people called Friends.

Sandy Really never had Friends before and was thrilled with the feeling. She spoke and they listened.

They spoke and she listened. Sometimes they disagreed. Sometimes they agreed. But always they smiled and shared and welcomed other's thoughts and feelings.

Sandy Really started learning more about life from these talks than she did from her mother or the men and women in long robes who taught her things from books.

Tom Twiddle was one of those Friends.

Tom Twiddle made a special effort to stand next to Sandy Really. Tom listened and agreed with everything Sandy said. Soon Sandy found herself alone with Tom and felt something she had never felt before. Tom was rich and smart, everything Mrs. Really had said Sandy Really wanted in a *Partner in Life*.

And before she knew it, Sandy Really became Mrs. Twiddle.

Mrs. Twiddle found herself in a beautiful house with no need for paint.

There were no cracks in the walls, inside or out. None in the sidewalks. No place to plant food or flowers.

There were other people in the house who took care of things like that.

Tom Twiddle forbade Mrs. Twiddle to paint, but he allowed her to cook. Mrs. Twiddle cooked the most incredible meals for Tom Twiddle. And he allowed her to sew, so she sewed the most elaborate robes for him.

He allowed her to clean, so she kept his house spotless and did everything her mother taught her to keep her *Partner in Life* happy.

And Tom Twiddle was happy.

But Mrs. Twiddle was not.

Nobody spoke to her anymore. No one listened to what she said. Not even Tom Twiddle.

Mrs. Twiddle felt lonely in her beautiful house full of people.

Mrs. Twiddle's fingers throbbed at the end of the day from mending Tom Twiddle's favorite clothes. Her back ached from polishing his floor into the shine he prided. Her hands wore blisters from making his favorite meals in the oven.

Mrs. Twiddle sat on the couch next to Tom Twiddle and snuggled up to his side. Tom Twiddle pushed her away and said the game was about over, but could she be a dear and get him a snack?

Yes, Mrs. Twiddle was a good *Partner in Life*, but Tom Twiddle was not.

The day came when she found herself back in the small rundown house in the middle of the small rundown field on the outskirts of the small rundown town in Wyoming.

She gave back Tom Twiddle's name and became Sandy Really once again.

Sandy Really liked being home at first. Then she grew sad and lonely. She missed the big, beautiful home she shared with Tom Twiddle. She yearned to talk with Friends again.

Mrs. Really saw her daughter's pain and told her to go to the city to find a job...and maybe a new and different *Partner in Life*.

A while ago...

But not yesterday...

Sandy Really set off for the big city. At first, she was afraid because she left the small rundown town on a small rundown bus, but as the bus got closer and closer to the big city, Sandy Really thought the city looked a lot like her old rundown town, only bigger...

Much bigger.

The bus station in the city was as rundown as the one in her rundown town, only bigger...

Much bigger.

Sandy Really found a small rundown apartment in the big city, next to a small rundown restaurant where she found a job. She went from table to table and got people what they asked for.

If they were nice people, they left her spare change. If they weren't, they left her nothing.

Luckily for Sandy Really, most of the people who ate at the restaurant were nice, and soon Sandy Really had a decent apartment, filled with little trinkets that made her smile.

In the small rundown restaurant next to her decent apartment worked a cook named Gary Greatest.

Sandy Really liked Gary Greatest. He made her laugh until she couldn't stand up. Gary Greatest lived in a decent apartment near hers, and soon they became good Friends. They went to the movies together and talked all night long about what Gary Greatest thought was right with the world. Sandy Really listened.

And like the last time, before she knew what happened Sandy Really turned into Mrs. Greatest.

Now, strange things happen to some people when they find themselves with any old *Partner in Life*. Mrs. Greatest knew Tom Twiddle had changed, but she never thought Gary Greatest would.

And yet, he did.

He liked to drink brown liquid from a bottle, and when he did it a lot, Gary Greatest became bad. Gary Greatest broke Mrs. Greatest's little trinkets. He shouted names at her and sold most of her things for more of the bottled brown liquid.

At night, Mrs. Greatest was not only sore from working, cooking, and cleaning, but also from bruises and marks Gary Greatest left on her when he had too much of the brown liquid. Mrs. Greatest was lonely. She didn't have anyone to talk to.

And, she was scared.

Once again, Sandy gave Gary Greatest back his name and became Sandy Really.

But Sandy Really didn't return to the small rundown house in the middle of the small rundown field on the outskirts of the small rundown town in Wyoming.

Instead, she found a nice apartment in a pretty part of the city and took a job working in a tall building down the block. She was smart, after all, and could use what she learned from college at her new job. She liked the people there and enjoyed talking with them.

She soon forgot all about Tom Twiddle and Gary Greatest.

Sandy Really worked hard at the job she loved and soon had a beautiful house of her own. It had no cracks, but she still painted flowers on the walls. She could afford curtains, but she sewed her own out of purple, green, and pink material anyway. She didn't need them, but she planted a garden of vegetables and grew flowers, too.

She let her hair wildly play upon her head and stopped covering her freckles with brown face paste.

Sandy Really was content for the first time since leaving her small rundown home in the middle of the small rundown field on the outskirts of the small rundown town in Wyoming.

Not yesterday...

But before...

Sandy Really wasn't looking for a *Partner in Life* anymore, but she met someone anyway.

Robbie Reliable worked next to Sandy Really in the big office building. They became good Friends and soon Robbie Reliable moved into Sandy Really's beautiful home.

This time, Sandy Really stayed Sandy Really.

And Robbie remained Reliable.

Robbie and Sandy both cooked when they wanted to eat. And they both cleaned when they needed to clean. They painted and planted and shared ideas. And they laughed together. And they smiled together. And sometimes they cried together... But not for long.

Robbie and Sandy's home glowed with love.

Sandy then understood what her mother meant when she told her to go out and find a *Partner in Life*. And Sandy knew Robbie was the right partner for her.

But to this day...

Yes, even yesterday...

Remarkably, she is still just Sandy.

Really.

**Originally published in *Diary of an Unkempt Woman*.

ABOUT THE AUTHOR

SANDRA MILLER LINHART

SANDRA MILLER LINHART WAS BORN in Lander, Wyoming on a warm summer day in a hospital which has since been turned into a mental institution... Which most likely holds no correlation... Probably.

Life inspires Sandra in both her writing and her art. Ms. Linhart holds degrees in Sociology, Paralegal, Writing, Graphic Arts, and Private Investigation. She's been featured on radio shows, invited to speak at schools, and participated in/facilitated conference panel discussions and presentations.

Sandra has five daughters, eight grandkids, and currently resides in the beautiful mountains of Wyoming.

Sandra Miller Linhart is an award-winning author and has been a member of the Society of Children's Book Writers and Illustrators (SCBWI), The Missouri Writer's Guild, and the Military Writers Society of America (MWSA).

Her award-winning titles include *Frozen Tears, Diary of an Unkempt Woman, Daddy's Boots, Don't Label Me, Mr. Gary Gots a Friend,* and *Pickysaurus Mac.*

Her titles can be found in online bookstores as well as libraries and brick-and-mortar bookstores. Visit her web page www.sandstarbooks.com

BLAZE OF GRACE

REGINA D'SCRIPTURA

WHEN THE MENTAL FOG OF disassociation lifted, she realized she'd made her way to the top of Billy Bump hill.

How in the world did I end up here? She realized she must have been wandering around in some sort of pseudo fugue state. She stood still for a moment, looking down at the valley below. A few of the Aspen trees were just starting to turn an orangish yellow, announcing crisp nights and cooler fall days. The breeze tussled her hair and brought with it a faint sour smell of the cow pastures east of town.

"Smells like money," her grandpa used to say.

Looking back over her left shoulder, she could just make out the top of the building she had for over nineteen years—until just a bit ago—called 'work'.

The box in her arms heavily weighed against her stomach as she realized she'd been carrying it for quite a while. Her muscles screamed in protest at being in the same position, the weight of the loaded box digging into her biceps and forearms. Her fingers felt numb.

I gotta sit down.

The well-worn gravel path she stood on was flanked by luscious green lawns. It looked as if it'd been recently mowed. So recently, she thought she might be catching the sweet scent of cut grass. *Maybe just a hint...* The thought of sitting on grass didn't please her at fifty-nine as much as it did when she was younger.

Her heart sank. In the beauty of the afternoon, she'd almost forgotten the mess she was in. Her legs faltered and she stumbled while standing.

"On your left." A trail bike whizzed past her, almost knocking her down. A fit young man in tight, purple-and-green spandex body glove and matching helmet peddled up the path and out of sight.

"Hey," she yelled. *That was rude. Damned near knocked me over. At least he's wearing proper attire. Wouldn't want to knock a pedestrian over wearing plain old silly clothes.*

"People are rude these days."

Startled, she looked toward the voice. A homeless older man sat on one side of a wrought-iron bench. His left hand rested on a shopping cart she presumed carried his belongings. He wore a long, dirty gray trench coat over a tattered brown-and-blue flannel shirt, dirty jeans and scuffed work boots. A white floppy cowboy hat covered most of the top of his head. With his long white beard and even longer white hair, if his coat were red and he weighed at least a hundred pounds more, he might have been mistaken for another jolly old man. He looked as if he hadn't showered in weeks.

"Correct term's 'unhoused' nowadays." He smiled at her, revealing a mouthful of pearly whites—all clean and perfectly straight—a complete dichotomy from his outward appearance. "Sit here." He motioned to the other side of the bench. "Ya look like you could use a rest."

She thought better of it, but her knees threatened to give out. She took a tentative step toward the bench with the unhoused man.

"Won't bite. Promise."

As she approached the bench, she contemplated placing the box on the ground beside her or between them. She didn't want to seem rude, but she also wasn't quite sure if he was at all safe. And she was exhausted.

"Ground's damp. Recently mowed, I think. Surprised, really... Comin' on about six, I'd guess." The man looked to the sun to solidify his claim. "Yep, 'bout six." With a sweep of his right hand, he pushed his jacket closer—seemingly to allow her more room on the other side of the bench.

He wasn't taking up too much space as he was a nimble, slight man. *Probably weighs less than me,* she thought as she placed the box between them and sat down. An audible sigh escaped her lips as she released the stress of the past few hours.

"Cookie?" The man held out what looked to be a chocolate-chip cookie.

She looked at it. *Chocolate chip? My favorite...*
Probably oatmeal raisin, knowing my luck today.
"No, thank you. But thank you, though."

He took a bite. "Oatmeal raisin isn't as good
a chocolate-chip, but one cookie is better than no
cookie, I suppose."

They sat in comfortable silence for a good bit.
Birds called in the surrounding bushes. Crickets
chirped from under the bench. The sounds of the busy
town drifted up from the left, cows lowing from the
right. A butterfly fluttered by on the breeze, nearly
settling on her hand before flitting off.

The relief from sitting and unburdening her arms
cast away all fears of the man beside her. *Besides,*
she thought. *If he wants to kill me, let him. What
else have I got to live for?*

"Now, that's not accurate," the man said, breaking the calm.

"Wha—?"

"Beautiful day, innut, Jay... Uh... Ma'am?" He
turned to her and stuck out his hand. "Name's Sam."

"Jane," she said. She hesitated before she shook
his hand. It was incredibly warm but not in a sickly
sense. For a flash of a moment, she felt like she'd
just come home, and then it was gone.

"What did you mean, 'it's not accurate'?"

"Oh, talkin' to m'self, I guess. There—over
the horizon. See how flat an' still that horizon is?
Gorgeous."

Jane looked where he pointed. She could see why the bench was placed there. One could look out and see for miles. The mountain range far in the distance to the right reminded her of the hikes she used to take in them.

"You know, there's a lake in the center of those mountains... I think that's about thirty-eight miles away as the crow flies..." Jane's finger pointed at the tallest peak.

"I know it. Lewis Lake. Great place to swim an' boat... An' fish. Campin' even. Used to do it a lot... A long time ago." Sam's eyes took on a dreamy, nostalgic look.

Jane examined Sam's face as he was lost in reverie.

"Do I know you?"

"Suppose so. Been 'round here all m'life. Mighta run inta me on occasion." Sam cleared his throat and came back to the present, it seemed. "Used ta have a cattle ranch down by the *Popo Agie*, down yonder. Had a mighty spread. Couple o' kids. Solid wife. Solid life."

"So, what happened? Why are you homel... Unhoused?"

Sam chuckled. "Can't take it with ya..." He turned to face her and indicated the box that sat between them. "Why are you... Unhoused?"

Jane had forgotten the box and its contents between the brief moments the two had shared. She looked down at it as if startled by its presence, and her heart sank remembering what the day had brought her.

"Oh, that. No. I'm still housed... For now, anyway. I just lost my job." She let out a stifled laugh. "Job. Sounds so irrelevant as a three-letter word...

"It was my life." Jane picked up a stapler. "And these... *Things*..." She tossed the stapler back into the box. "Are all I have left of the life I devoted almost twenty years to. And the kicker? They made me redundant just two months before I became eligible for retirement." Tears welled up in Jane's eyes as her shoulders slumped as self-pity and despair overtook her.

What am I going to do, now? She watched as the sun slowly grew smaller and closer to the apparent horizon while she considered her options. She secretly wanted it all to go away. Just give up the ghost and all let her worries disappear like the soon-setting sun. Silence filled the void, and the sounds of nature gently filled the silence.

For the third time in her life, Jane felt a deep and overwhelming despair from her situation. Only two other times had she felt so abandoned and alone. The first time was when she got the news her parents had been killed by a drunk driver in a car crash on their way home from her college graduation. She never really forgave herself for that. Neither did her sister, who cut all ties with her after their funerals.

The second time—

"Never wanted to be a rancher." Sam's revelation interrupted Jane's memories. "Thought I'd live a life o' excitement an' danger. Hunting an' trappin' the expanses o' Alaska. Maybe rushin' fer gold in the mountains o' Colorada. Yep. Live fast, die young was the motto. Go out in a blaze o' glory, as it were."

"What happened?"

Sam's lip wistfully turned up in a half smile. "Found grace instead. Met my Cora. Tamed me, she did. All that so-called excitement paled in comparison to her bright blue eyes."

Sam slapped his hands down on his thighs, startling Jane. "Nope," he said. "No regrets. Now. What kind o' job did ya say you lost?"

"Paralegal."

"Why'd ya love it?"

"I, uh... I loved the research. The diving in and making a difference. Shedding truth on the lies and exposing the darkness to light." Jane's rush of words faltered, and her face grew flushed. "I know it may sound overly dramatic and maybe boring for some, but I really enjoyed the puzzle of it and the precise writing of motions to compel the court."

"How'd ya lose it?"

"Our new District Attorney... She was just sworn in a few months ago. I liked her. She seemed smart and honest. Then, I started to see how deceptive she was... Is. And I had a really hard time respecting her. She gave favors to people who had contributed to her election campaign—letting things slide, writing off minor traffic tickets.

"When I questioned her on a case she dismissed out of court, she grew angry and threw me out of her office. She wrote me up for insubordination."

Jane took a moment to collect her thoughts before continuing. "So... For the next couple of days, I did some deep digging and found out the child abuse case she dismissed... The perp is her nephew. I brought it to the attention of my ADA this morning. When my discovery went up the chain, a pink slip came down, and I was out the door by five. No good deed, I suppose..."

"What did ya hope to gain by rattin' her out?"

"Ratting her... No, I wasn't '*ratting her out*'. It's illegal, what she did. If she's supposed to uphold the law, she shouldn't feel above it." Jane felt anger rise inside as her cheeks grew warm. She tightly pulled her sweater around her for comfort and protection.

"Ya never done nothin' illegal?" Sam's left eyebrow raised a little higher than his right.

"Well, sure... Yeah. Sped. I go over the speed limit all the time."

"You feel above the law?"

"No! If I got caught, I'd pay the ticket."

"If?"

"Well, yeah..."

"So, it's okay as long as ya don't get caught." Sam chuckled.

Jane's frustration overtook her, and she felt her voice rise. "If you can sit here and compare letting a child molester go free to going five miles over the speed limit, then, sir, I don't know what to tell you. We live in two very different worlds."

"Aye, that we do, miss. Didn't mean to ruffle yer feathers." Sam's warm smile and slight apology calmed Jane's ire a bit. "Who wrote those law books you're so keen on?"

"We did, I guess."

"We? Me an' you?"

"No. Man. Men. People."

"And what good are they, these laws?"

"What do you mean? They keep people in check, you know, doing the right thing. Not infringing on others." Jane's voice had risen an octave. She reminded herself to calm down. She fussed with a tissue in her sweater pocket. Wiped at her nose and replaced it.

"People need laws to keep 'em in check, now do they?"

"Yes."

"So, the only thing keepin' you from killin' me an' takin' my stuff is there're laws agin it?"

"No! I wouldn't kill anyone. Ever! Or take their stuff."

Sam smiled.

"Yer job give you a sense o' somethin'? Of belongin' or pride, or...?"

"Yeeaahhh... I guess. I felt needed. Necessary. Important, maybe. No. Relevant. It made me feel relevant."

Sam nodded his head as if he understood.

"We all need ta feel relevant, I suppose." After a slight pause, "You got a family? Husband? Kids?"

"Once upon a time, yeah."

"What happened there?" Sam's face grew concerned as he looked into Jane's eyes.

A warm breeze picked up and stirred the branches of a nearby bush, giving Jane a reason to look away. She felt her lower eyelids fill as a tingling started in her nose. A single tear betrayed her. She silently wiped it away and cleared her throat.

"My parents both died when I was twenty-two—car crash. I have an older sister who, um. Uh, and... Gregory. My husband's name was Gregory. *Is* Gregory. I met him just after college. We were married for about fifteen years about twenty years ago. We had... *Have* two daughters—now both grown adults with kids of their own." Jane wiped another errant tear from her face. "He's happily living in Michigan with his new, uh, younger wife, Trudy, and their two kids."

"What happened to yer girls?"

"They never forgave me for not fighting harder for my marriage. Said I didn't try hard enough or love deep enough." Jane sniffled and wiped her eyes. "Who knows? They're probably right. I couldn't feel past the betrayal I felt. I couldn't find forgiveness in my heart for the longest time. And when I could, and did, it was too late. I'd lost them all."

"Have ya reached out to 'em? Bridged the gap?"

"I've tried. I send them letters, birthday cards, Christmas cards... I've only seen pictures of my grandkids. I send them cards, too. But I've yet to get any response. I hope someday they'll reach back. I trust someday they will. I hope. I keep the door open." Jane sighed. "So, for the longest time it's been just me and my dog, Rodger."

"So, then, you gave yer all to yer job?"

"For all the good it did."

"Now, I'm sure ya did some good where you could. An' ya put yer heart an' soul in 'er. Don't you fret about that." Sam put his hand on Jane's shoulder, comforting her. She felt no desire to pull away. Instead, she fought off the strange and sudden urge to fall into his arms and weep. Tears clouded her eyes.

"I'll never know. I can only hope. Now, I have to figure out what I'm going to do."

"What d'ya wanna do? What sings to yer soul an' makes yer ticker pump?"

Jane thought for a moment before answering. "Art." *But you can't make a living off art.*

"Who says ya can't?"

"Can't what?" *Did I say that out loud?*

"Make a livin' off it. And ya didn't need to. Understand more than you think, I do."

"Can you read my mind?" Jane looked at the man. There was something oddly familiar about him. He was dressed in raggy soiled clothing, but smelled woodsy, like Siberian Fir with a blend of Cedar. His face seemed like it was wrinkled... It should have been wrinkled but wasn't—it radiated a translucent glow just underneath the skin.

"Read yer mind? What a silly notion that is. Can I tell ya a story?"

Sam didn't wait for Jane's reply. He rummaged through his shopping cart and pulled out an old rag doll. She had red yarn hair, a cloth face and body, and wore a blue-and-white plaid dress with ruffles and a white apron. She had two button eyes and an unfaltering painted smile on her face.

"Me an' my Cora had two daughters o' our own, barely two years apart in age. When the oldest was 'bout three, I'd say, she'd seen a rag doll in the *Sear's* Christmas catalogue. Ow, man, she wanted that baby doll bad. She asked her momma with such sweetness an' politeness to please buy her that baby. Nearly broke my heart."

Sam's sparkling eyes seemed to search out the sun. Jane's eyes followed his and found it just reaching the horizon. *About an hour... Forty-five minutes maybe until dusk*, Jane figured.

Sam continued.

"Ranchin' is a harsh mistress. One day you're on top o' the mountain. The next, yer deep in the trenches, tryin' to scrape enough food together fer a meal. At that point 'n time, me an' the missus had little to spare—nothin' fer a store-bought baby, no matter how much we wanted to. After a recent harsh blizzard, we'd lost half our herd—we thought we'd lose the farm an' all we'd worked so hard fer. As much as she hated to, Cora had to tell our little one, 'no'."

Jane patiently waited while Sam mentally relived the past moments for a while. She watched the sun's bottom edge touch the apparent horizon. After a bit, he spoke again.

"Ruthie stood tall with a tremblin' lower lip an' said to her momma, 'I understand.' She climbed into her momma's hug an' never shed one tear over the baby in that catalogue. Well, you can imagine, *that* near to broke my missus' heart.

"Christmas mornin' came an' with it came two packages under the tree—one fer Ruthie an' one fer her baby sister. When the wrappin' paper came off, Ruthie found this little doll in her arms." Sam held up the rag doll. "She isn't as bright as the doll in the catalogue, an' she has no red on her. But, Ruthie's face wore a look o' pure love when she snuggled this doll, an' then her momma."

As the evening cooled, a strange, dense fog bank rose from the east pasture, creeping in as the sun receded, along with the songs of nature.

"Just like our Creator, we want the best fer our children. All they need do is ask, and we'll do everythin' within our power to grant their heart-felt wishes. Sometimes we can. Other times, we can't or shouldn't. There's no difference between him..." Sam pointed up to the sky. "And us, when it comes to our children."

"Ya see, Cora had spent ever' night that month hand sewin' two dolls from old clothin' an' rags—a girl doll fer Ruthie, an' a boy doll fer Ruthie's sister, Suzie." Sam held out the rag doll for Jane.

"My mom's name was Suzie. What a sweet coincidence," Jane said, taking the doll.

"I don't believe in coincidences... At any rate, Ruthie and Suzie never wandered far from their baby dolls that weren't quite o' the catalogue variety, and Cora Jane never wandered far from them.

"He sent me here to tell ya, you are never alone. He doesn't wander far from you, and he's been keepin' that door open... Follow yer dreams, Jane. Everythin' happens fer a reason, an' you've been given a clean slate. You can be whatever ya want—to achieve whatever you desire. Live life with grace and do it in love." Sam stood and pulled his cart to the front of him.

A strong breeze wafted between them, swirling the fog and bringing the overwhelming sour smell of a nearby cow pasture—full force and repulsive.

"Smells like money," Sam said. He winked at Jane, turned, and disappeared into the fog.

ABOUT THE AUTHOR

REGINA D'SCRIPTURA

REGINA D' SCRIPTURA HOLDS DEGREES in Writing, Sociology, and Graphic & Commercial Arts. She's been featured on radio shows, invited to speak at schools, and has participated in numerous conference panel discussions and presentations.

Regina lives in Wyoming with her wiener dog, Rodger. They camp, hike, and enjoy nature whenever they can. Life inspires Regina in both her writing and her art.

Regina's short stories and articles have been published in many quarterly magazines. This is her second submission to an anthology. Her first is included in *Ripples, an Anthology*.

DEADHEAD ROSES

DUSTY FACINELLI-JANISCH

A T THAT POINT IN HIS life, Daniel's prevailing anxiety was *Fitting In*. After all, it was the first quarter of senior year in a new high school at the dawn of the millennium and his classmates were ruthless.

Daniel rose, quickly and quietly, to a cold dark house. Rubbing his eyes, he felt around in the blackness for his bundled sheets. Grabbing the corners, he threw up the fold and snapped the edges straight over the bed like a pro, landing them with precision.

Gliding in the shadows, he grabbed a trendy button-down shirt and denim jeans—ones he'd set out the night before. On his way out of the room, a sliver of moonlight revealed a glimpse of his younger brother's blissful face, dead asleep under a wall plastered with *Green Day* posters.

Sleeping in as long as possible I see. Must be nice. I bet he wears the same thing as yesterday. God, I miss my old room... Daniel rolled his eyes on the way out the door and silently maneuvered down the unlit hallway.

Flipping on the bathroom light, his chocolate-brown eyes squinted in a hiss from the blinding contrast. His thoughts compiled as his stark image stared back from the mirror.

Okay. How bad is it today?

He groaned, analyzing his reflection inches from the mirror. One hand propped himself up against the pale tile countertop while his other hand's long fingers gently traced in detection mode over his budding, teenage face—careful and deliberate, more concentrated than if he were fluent in braille.

Hmm... Not bad for once. Skin's looking pretty clear. Okay. Today's going to be a good day after all. His mouth curled into a half shocked semi-smile.

Not fully convinced his eyes weren't deceiving him, he gave himself one last glance over, looking for any more possible unsightly protrusions.

But, wow. This hair!

His hands ruffled his head, trying to tame the disheveled mess, reminding him of its resilience.

Ugh. Time for that shower.

Daniel took pride in putting himself together every morning, never letting anyone see his bushy brown hair without a good soaking. He also always got up earlier than everyone else for a few reasons but mostly to hide the fact he took the longest to get ready. He'd never admit that to anyone, of course.

Shampooing his head, hot water splashed over his athletic build as the downpour invited a thousand thoughts swirling:

Am I really wearing that shirt? Or is it too much? Those are my good jeans at least... And what is taking so long with the audition results? I wonder if they liked me. I mean, Dean nailed his part, but did I?

Rinsing and conditioning his hair, more dissonant thoughts compiled.

Don't forget you have a Chemistry exam first period, and she asked you to study with her beforehand. Wait, did I finish all the homework? Ugh! This week is never ending. Thank God it's Friday...

Just about finished with his last rinse, his attention being pulled—

Chemistry... Dean will be there. I can't believe we got paired up for that scene... Everything about him is so perfect. How is that even possible... God, I wish I had his hair.

Okay, Whatever. Time to get going. You need to make breakfast.

Finished, he shut off the water and stepped out of the shower feeling refreshed. Unconsciously humming, scents of cucumber and melon permeated the air as he dressed and reviewed the results in the mirror, sighing in submission.

This shirt is fine. You just wore your favorite outfit the other day...

Okay, time to get this hair right... His well-trained hands did their best to towel dry with precision, grabbed a wad of hair wax, and smoothed the sides of his head like a potter—doing everything they could to get "the look".

Finally accepting there was only so much he could do, his wrists and biceps begging to acquiesce when—

BANG! BANG!

"Daniel! Hurry up in there," screeched a disgusted voice.

His arms dropped, allowing a rush of blood to flow back down in relief. Hurrying, he washed the remnants of the sticky pomade from his hands, gave himself one last glance over—finally with approval, and flung the door open to his stepsister's ominous presence.

"Hey, sorry. All yours," he said, shuffling past her without making eye contact down the stairs to an empty kitchen. He knew better. Plus, he visualized her eye roll through the closed door—he didn't want to give her any satisfaction.

In the mornings he made his own breakfast, always making a little extra—filling two plates with bright yellow scrambled eggs, strips of crispy bacon, and warm pieces of wheat toast buttered with care and topped with a dollop of Grandma's famous apricot jam.

Singing to himself, he popped the last bit of toast into his mouth and moved his dirty dishes and pans to the sink, giving them a quick rinse before loading the dishwasher.

He carried the second plate down the hall.

Knock, knock

He uttered a gentle, "Good morning, Grandma. I have your breakfast," as he slowly let himself in.

"Oh, good morning, Daniel." The scent of sizzled bacon preceded him as he made his way to her bedside. "Perfect timing, sweetie."

Their eyes connected with a soft smile.

"Getting taller and more handsome every day, I see." She repositioned herself further.

He smiled. "How are you feeling?" His eyebrows lifted in genuine concern.

"Don't get old dear," she whipped with a quick laugh. Finally wiggling her shoulders to the top of her pillows, cracking a smile she eyed her breakfast and added, "Oh, this smells lovely, Daniel."

After the initial bite, she paused. "Mm... Delicious, thank you." She closed her eyes with bliss mid chew. Opening them to look Daniel in the eye, she asked, "So, how do you like your new school?"

"It's fine, Grandma. No complaints." His words sounded hollow, even to him.

"That's good..." She took another bite, pausing. "And how are your school mates? I know it's got to be hard switching your senior year. Making new friends, I hope?" She finished the bite and put her fork down.

Daniel looked at the floor. Dean popped into his mind, quickly followed by the pretty girl who sat beside him in Chemistry class. He shrugged.

"Hmm... Well, maybe we'll get to see you in another production this winter. I know how much you loved that at your last school." Warm encouragement coated her voice.

"We'll see, Grandma. I don't know yet... I auditioned a few days ago for a musical but don't tell Dad. He isn't happy I quit football—"

"Oh, rubbish! Don't let that sourpuss dampen your spirit. You're a special boy, Daniel. And talented! Your mom would be so proud." One hand emphasized her words in the air while the other steadily held her plate.

"You know, grandmas tell it like it is," she said with deliberate emphasis, pointing with her eyes and index finger at his face. That time their eyes met with a warm ping to his heart.

"Thanks, Grandma," he murmured, looking down again, dreading the thought of being a "special" boy.

He appreciated the sentiment, though. At least someone acknowledges her, he thought, remembering his late mother who always encouraged his acting pursuits.

"So, tell me. What scene did you perform?" Grandma asked with genuine curiosity.

"Oh. It was *Poor Jud is Dead*." A memory of his audition with Dean flashed and brought a gentle smile to his face.

"*OKLAHOMA!* I love that musical. Reminds me of my time in the South." Grandma's laugh tickled his ears. "And what role are you hoping for?"

"Jud."

"Really!? I picture you more like a Curly, Will, or even Ike, myself." She said with a playful wink and a grin. "But, okay. Jud, it is. You do have a beautiful voice, dear."

Daniel lifted his gaze to meet hers and shyly smiled. "Thank you... Okay, well. Do you need anything else? I should probably get going." He quickly stood up, hoping to deter any further questions. "Cheryl is taking us all now that Bianca and I go to the same school. They're probably almost ready."

Commotion billowed from beyond the walls, causing them to look toward the door.

"Cheryl. I see..." Grandma's upper lip crinkled to her nose with a side eye to match. "So, your father hasn't given you the truck yet, eh?" She asked, keeping him for a moment longer. "You know you can borrow my car anytime you'd like. God knows it needs to be driven."

"Thanks, Grandma. We'll see."

He mentally shook the image of an old rusty champagne-colored *Buick* from his mind. Even though he felt like the only senior in school without his own car, he had his limits.

"Okay. Well... I bet they're waiting for me. We're picking up Bianca's new boyfriend now, too."

Their eyes rolled in unison as they gave each other a quick smirk. He bent over to kiss her on the forehead, not wanting to detain the ice queens, when he noticed his grandma's attention shift out the window.

"Don't they look marvelous?" A mature bush of gorgeous pink, white, and yellow roses swayed in the view. "You've been keeping up with them really well, but it's about time again," she added.

Daniel looked out the window, his heart gleaned a sense of pride for them.

"Oh my!" She laughed. "I will never forget the fuss you made when I first taught you how to dead-head the roses. Bless your heart. I can still hear you..." She chuckled. "'But Grandma, why!?' You moaned in utter bewilderment—wide eyed and precious watching the beautiful blossoms fall to the floor. Oh, boy. You were fine with me snipping the wilted, but your poor little mind could not make sense of the still 'pretty' ones.

"You were such a sweet boy..."

"I know, I know, Grandma." He cracked a smile. "I'll get around to it, I prom—"

"OKAY! TIME TO GO!" Bianca's drill-sergeant shriek penetrated the walls, disrupting the calm inside Grandma's room.

They both looked to the door as Grandma's hand gently grabbed his wrist, sending a sensation of grace straight to his heart.

"You're going to get the part, I know it," She predicted.

But Daniel was already in motion. Her hand slipped off his, taking the comforting feeling with it as he headed out the door. Walking off, he looked back as he closed the door behind him, catching one last glimpse of care.

"LET'S GOOO!" Bianca screeched from the garage, claiming the backseat—which was odd for her.

Opening the front passenger side, Daniel said, "Hi, good morning, Cheryl," doing his best to be cordial.

His stepmom didn't reply. Which was like her—something always seemed to be on her mind.

"Hey, Buddy! Watch the buckles on your backpack," Cheryl squawked as Daniel settled into his seat. As soon as the rattle of the garage door finished lifting, she blindly backed the SUV out and onto the street. "I don't want you to scratch the interior," she added, glaring at him.

Cheryl looked like a modern big-eyed and beak-nosed evil stepmother from *Cinderella* who'd just asked for the "Rachel" haircut from *Friends*.

Daniel looked down, confirming his backpack was secured between his feet, clearly doing no harm. He did not let her tone bother him and was just about to open his mouth to try and engage in conversation again when—

"We can't be late," Bianca announced.

Compared to her mother Bianca hit the genetic lottery, but unfortunately her scrunched nose and pointy eyes always looked like she caught a whiff of something foul she couldn't shake.

"Brock is already waiting for us. I cannot wait to see him!" She cackled to herself like a witch. "Mom! Did I tell you I found out he's going to ask me to Homecoming!? Oh my God. Captain of the cheer squad with a varsity football junior. We are going to be so cute."

Oh, God. Of course. Can she hear herself? Daniel rolled his eyes out of sight of mother and daughter.

Moments later as they approached Brock's street, Bianca gasped, "Oh! And he's getting his license in like two weeks. He said he's going to get a new *Mustang* and start driving me to school. How cool will that be!?"

"Oh, gooood. Then I won't have to drive any-more." Cheryl fake laughed as she pulled the car over, and then with a smirk added, "But I guess that means you, Daniel, will have to start taking the school bus. Shame."

Before Daniel could react, Bianca took back the conversation.

"There he is!" she shrieked. As she giddily bounced up and down in the back seat. "He looks so good today." Gushing.

Daniel looked out the window to a tall, chis-eled-looking teenage boy—his well-fitting jeans and T-shirt popped with muscley bumps in all the right places as he walked like an *Abercrombie* model toward their car, seemingly in slow motion.

Daniel immediately recognized Brock from their brief time together on the football team.

"Okay, here he comes. Don't embarrass me," Bianca hissed.

Brock opened the car door.

"Hey, babe," Bianca's seductive coo was soon followed by Cheryl's warmer than usual, "Good morning, Brock," sounding too similar to her daughter's purr.

That was weird. Wow, she must really want to be a young grandma. Daniel suppressed a chuckle.

"Hey, good morning, Mrs. Masters," Brock said in a deep voice. Piling into the back seat, he followed with, "Hey... Daniel? Right?"

"Hey, how's it going? ...Brock?" Daniel responded dropping his tone deeper than usual to match Brock's, acting as if he didn't really recognize him, either.

Picking up on the fact Brock's attention moved on as quickly as it came, Daniel turned to stare out the front passenger window again, knowing he was already being ignored.

"Brock!" Bianca screamed, causing Daniel to involuntarily look back in surprise.

Brock's big hands squeezed her tight on the soft sides of her thin waist, pulling her in for a kiss on the lips. The two giggled in unison while Daniel's skin crawled, and his ears craved an ice pick.

"Okay, you two, buckle up," Cheryl laughed as she pulled the car into the street.

Daniel turned his attention back to the view from his window, trying to ignore why he felt so annoyed while continuing to hide his facial expressions.

The typical suburban neighborhood rushed by in a blur under a blanket of melancholy gray clouds.

Reluctant to say much to anyone, Daniel remained silent as his stepmom drove the three of them to school.

"Stop it, Brock!" Bianca laughed. "Doooon't!" She screeched like an obnoxious damsel-in-distress. Her squeals and giggles permeated the car—most annoyingly over the pop radio.

Daniel did his best to ignore them, but their obvious attempts for attention were getting to be a bit much. He visualized Cheryl unblinkingly staring at the road with a permanent smirk on her face—one he rarely saw—indicating she did not mind the PDA one bit.

Daniel stole a glance her way and found his thoughts vindicated. She wore a half-cocked smile and a dazed stare as if she were enjoying the back-seat antics.

You've got to be kidding me. She's okay with this? They're like fifteen. How far have they gone?

His only escape was entertaining himself with his thoughts, staring out the passenger-side window.

He must've heard Cheryl say, 'Bianca made captain of the cheer squad' in her nasally voice a thousand times. Could be anywhere. The grocery store checkout. The bank teller window. The dentist. Most people typically found small talk redundant, but not that mom. She was vehemently proud of her cheerleader daughter.

WOW. She IS the definition of living vicariously. And how fitting, Bianca's dating one of the best-looking guys in school...

Whatever, he thought, feeling more annoyed every minute. He started to realize how he was coming off and forced himself to shake the feeling, aware Cheryl was more than likely picking up on his increasingly aloof energy and analyzing his reactions. He knew not participating in the "fun" wouldn't go unnoticed. Not placating wasn't smart.

Feeling obligated and just to save face, Daniel tilted his head back and cracked a smile with a laugh like, *Oh, you two,* avoiding all eye contact.

A quick whip of the head and back to staring out the window, his fake smile faded quicker than last. Taking his gaze off the side of the road as it whizzed past, he sensed they were getting close.

Almost there... Just another few minutes stuck in this damn car... *sigh* Until the real hell begins, but at least I might get to hang with Dean... And, God, I wish I could turn up this song!

Don't admit that! You don't really want to listen to it, do you? Ask them to turn it to K-ROCQ.

...but you don't want that either...

"And that was the new smash single, *Crazy,* by Britney Spears."

Ugh! The bus? Maybe I should take Grandma up on her offer...

Yes, then you can listen to whatever you want.

Don't think about that. Besides, you can't show up in that old POS... But anything is better than the bus. You're a senior! His thoughts torturing him, he tried to block it all and zone out to the radio.

Sensing they were getting close to school, he intuitively noticed more red lights taking longer and packed pedestrians' crossings. Their SUV pulled behind a bright yellow school bus centered mere feet in front of them, awaiting the green turn-arrow light.

Shuffling through thoughts, he replayed the scene he and Dean auditioned, just getting to the part where—

"Oh! My! God! Look!" Bianca leaned in and stuck her arm between him and Cheryl, pointing to the front windshield.

Daniel reactively looked out and up, only able to see the back of the yellow bus.

And there it was.

Without warning.

On a simple sheet of white paper were the six letters, FAGGOT staring back in bold black caps— unapologetically plastered across the back window.

Time.

Suddenly.

Stood.

Still.

Daniel's stomach pulled inward in agony, as if sucker punched in the gut.

Holding a blank expression tight, his head tilted up as though he was rapidly falling in an elevator.

Looking at the roof of the car, all he could process was Cheryl's stunned guffaw and a few approving chuckles from the back seat.

A heat wave of embarrassment instantaneously engulfed him, flushing his body—which was retaliating in full panic mode inside, dying to escape.

THAT did not just happen!

He lowered his head for a moment, trying to avoid the sign but unable to escape a second look.

FAGGOT simply stared back. Still without remorse.

Daniel blinked twice in an attempt to register and erase the image, but then he squinted, desperate curiosity took over and he shifted his focus to what he could see through the slightly tinted windows.

Two punky-looking boys appeared, each pressing a side of the sign against the window with one hand and pointing at their SUV with the other, hysterically laughing.

DO NOT react. Heat enshrouded every inch of his skin.

Doing his best to look unbothered, he repositioned himself in the seat—sitting straight-up and frozen.

The inferno traversed Daniel's body as a pit in his stomach took root and quickly sprouted, moving the flushed feeling from his entire face to burning behind his eyes. Unable to avoid the situation, he turned and stared out his side window disassociating, not daring to read the sign again.

Then, out of the corner of his eye, he saw the paper vanish just as stealthily as it appeared. But, the damage was already done.

The various reactions within the car revealed how truly unempathetic the other passengers were, and their apathy began to suffocate him.

This can't be happening.

The lift of the brakes provided a false sense of relief as their car inched forward through the green light. Still trailing behind the bus like metal chasing a magnet, they followed in silence toward the school's drop-off curb. Daniel remained tight-chested and expressionless.

Cheryl pulled the car to the curb and parked a foot behind the bus, ostensibly on purpose. Daniel's intense stillness formed sweat beads across his brow and upper lip. Without a word or a glance, he calmly opened the door, grabbed his backpack, and closed the car door behind him with semi-composure.

The ominous yellow bus seemed double its size, seizing his peripheral.

He outwardly stumbled a few steps—like he had spaghetti strings for legs and two left shoes—trying to find footing. Before he felt like anyone noticed, he managed to compose himself, finally able to exhale and lift his head high—acting as if the offending poster was not meant for him.

I have to get away from here.

After a few solid steps the asphyxiated feeling of judgmental eyes laughing at his back reverberated through his body as he attempted a wispy inhale, his lungs barely expanded with the breath. The chill of the cold draft from the car chastised him as a roar of laughter echoed in his mind, rattling him to his core.

Don't you cry. He bemoaned, feeling heat intensify back behind his eyes. A pounding in his chest propelled his steps faster.

Don't you fucking cry, he pleaded—begging his body not to turn on him in front of anyone as fresh tears pierced through against his will.

As he distanced, retreating from it all, his legs strengthened. Picking up the pace, he walked as fast and calmly as he could toward the school doors—sensing the school bus was nearly empty by that time.

His vision blurred. *No. No! This can't be happening.* Tilting his head up toward the sky, he fought back the tears with all his might.

I have to find a bathroom. I cannot be seen like this.

Hurrying forward, he entered the school blurry eyed and took a blind turn down the first hall toward the nearest restroom.

Steps from the men's room door, Cheryl flashed into mind.

She doesn't even care about me at all. He intensely felt the sting of her heartlessness. *She's probably going to take this personally. 'This is your mother's doing,' she'll say.*

Bianca's squeaky voice chimed in next with, *'And then he just sat there dumbfounded saying nothing.*

It was so awkward. I mean, how embarrassing.' Her approving chuckles from the back seat rang in his ears as he pushed through the bathroom door still balancing a well of tears.

Does she think putting me down somehow lifts herself up? I cannot stand her.

And great, then there's Brock. I am so embarrassed.

Then, it happened.

A droplet broke free, lost down his cheek.

He'll probably tell everyone on the football team, and they'll think that's why I quit.

Flinging the back of his hand up like swatting a fly, he erased the tear and beelined past the few guys using the urinals toward the stall doors.

What assholes. He pushed open the nearest stall, escaping inside. He slammed the door shut, latching it tight. More phantom laughter singed his eardrums as mental images of a bus full of kids howling took over his mind.

Why were they saying that?

More tears amassed, free to gather.

He pictured those boys and all the school cliques masquerading around like a little militia, asserting dominance with every sideways glance. Laughing. At him.

And how'd they even do that so fast? Shaking his head in disbelief. *Were we sitting there that long? Did they know it was me?* His defenses only able to hold off for so long when—

Oh, my God! What is Dad going to think? Feeling like he was at his lowest point, the knot in his stomach doubled as he stood there. His stomach twisted an agonizing notch causing him to sit on the edge of the toilet seat. Behind the closed door, the dam holding back his tears finally burst.

He's going to want to know why. Warm tears streamed down his cheeks like rain drops, silently splattering between his feet in all directions on the tile floor.

Everyone knows. No one likes you. Your mom is dead, you disgusting worthless—FAGGOT. The word flashed back like lightning.

Shaking in disbelief he just sat there, wet faced and miserable.

In truth, Daniel didn't really know what he was... Or wasn't. Everything was new, including growing up.

Contrasting and contradicting emotions tumbled and whirled inside him all at once. Loss, excitement, embarrassment, confusion, infatuation, disgust, hate, despair—all too intertwined to make sense of, and all pointing to one simple conclusion—

Without warning, the school bell rang. Alarmingly faster than he was expecting.

No! I can't take this...

Do I have to go? Maybe I can be excused for personal reasons? But he knew, for boys there was not that option.

Aw, crap! You were supposed to meet with her before class to study for the exam.

Forcing himself to find composure, he remained motionless a moment longer to focus his hearing for any signs of life outside his enclosure. He glanced around for feet under the stall doors. Relieved to be alone, he exited into an empty bathroom. The temporary relief forced him to glance in the mirror.

God, you look terrible.

Diverting his eyes down to the faucet handles, he turned on the sink to regroup, finding a balance with the water temperature.

I am not giving anyone the satisfaction of seeing me like this. I especially don't want Dean to see me like this, either... He splashed warm water on his face. *I know he drives himself to school, so he couldn't have heard anything... Yet, at least. God, I hope not. Maybe he won't even hear about this at all. Those boys had to have been juniors... Or even younger...* attempting to reassuringly convince himself nobody his grade could possibly know what had happened.

He dried his face and fluffed his hair, managing to get it back in line.

Standing at the bathroom door, he took a deep inhale to calm his nerves, and, with his exhale, burst through the door and took off to class like nothing had happened.

Ding!

Daniel squeezed into his seat just as the tardy bell silenced.

His neighbor, the pretty blond girl with bright green eyes didn't hold back her concern. "Hey, I was waiting for you. Where were you?" she asked, as the last of the stragglers took their seats. "You okay?" she whispered.

Silent, his lips pulled in and tightened. He looked away from her, catching a glimpse of Dean's perfect face from across the room. They made quick eye contact, as if saying hello.

"Okay, class. Get out a pen and paper for the exam." Their teacher captured the attention of the room.

With a click and a clack, he lit up the projector like he had done a million times, indifferent of anyone's emotions, illuminating several bold lettered words and equations that, again, blankly stared back at everyone.

Everything moved in slow motion as Daniel's mind disappeared into a dizzying fog. He tore out a piece of notebook paper, picked up his pencil, and stared at the paper as his mind wandered—into deep contemplation—the morning's event on loop in his mind.

"Okay, pencils down. Hand your paper to your neighbor for grading."

"Daniel, you didn't write anything..." said the green-eyed girl, relaying concern.

"It's fine," his breath catching just above his heart. "I've just got a lot on my mind. Sorry about this morning..." Attempting to process his way out of the nightmare, it hit him.

"Hey!" His voice came out louder than intended and she startled a bit at his enthusiasm. He regulated his voice and asked, "Do you want to go out tomorrow?" He leaned in close and finally looked into her eyes.

"Yeah, let's do it." Her face lit up at the idea.

"Okay, cool. I'll pick you up at noon. We can hang at the mall, grab a bite... Or something." He momentarily felt relieved and slumped back into his chair.

Time on stand still finally resumed.

"Okay... So, I'll see you tomorrow?" The green-eyed girl's blond hair and soft features paused, staring at him for confirmation moments after the bell dismissed class.

"Oh, uh, yeah," His earlier bravado fading with each passing second.

"Okay, great!" She handed him a small, folded piece of paper with a delicate flower sketched on the front. "Here's my phone number and address. So sorry. I have to rush off, but I'm looking forward to it. To you." She winked.

Dean bumped into her as he approached Daniel's desk, catching Daniel by surprise as he put his binder into his backpack.

"Hey, Daniel. How's it going?"

"Oh, hey. What's up?" Daniel's voice nearly cracked.

"Guess what I heard?"

Daniel's heart seized. *Please God. Please let him not know about this morning.*

"They're posting the cast list after school today, outside the theater." Dean's blue eyes sparkled with excitement. "Meet you there?"

Oh, thank God. Lost in Dean's eyes a moment, Daniel felt his breath catch, then recovered. "Yes. For sure. Sounds good."

"Okay, great! See you there." Dean took off with a pep in his step toward the far side of campus.

Daniel watched him leave, feeling excited that Dean came up to him first, but uneasy about the try-out results.

By last period, he had ridden a roller coaster of emotions, anticipating and preparing for the multiple scenarios headed his way. *Dad is going to kill me... But, I wonder if we got the parts...* Daniel watched the minute hand tick over until it triggered the last bell for the day, freeing everyone for the weekend.

On his way to the theater, he stopped by the bathroom to check his hair and face, making sure everything looked in place. Keeping a side glance for anyone who may have witnessed that morning's hell, he felt mild relief, like it must be old news already but still uneasy about it.

Maybe everyone will have forgotten about this morning by Monday... Making his way across campus, *Okay, there's the theater...*

He noticed Dean's blond hair tussled by the breeze. *And there he is.*

"WE GOT THEM!" Dean waved and yelled in Daniel's direction from yards away.

Daniel rushed over to the board. His eyes and finger scanning the OKLAHOMA! cast list, trailing down. Dean's name in all caps caught his eye first followed with his a few names down.

CURLY—DEAN JOHNSTON

JUD FRY—DANIEL MASTERS

His heart skipped a beat.

"No way! This is great!" Daniel laughed, making eye contact with Dean. The two almost hugged mid excitement but Daniel quickly offered a fist bump, which Dean returned. Amid the exhilaration, the pit hanging out in Daniel's stomach kicked his insides like it was a fetus.

"Hey, why don't we go get a bite to celebrate? I can drop you off at home after," Dean suggested.

Daniel's heart fluttered.

"Sounds great," he said, keeping his composure.

He quickly pulled his phone out and scrolled down to BIANCA. An anxious wave washed over him. He noticed his hand shaking as he sent the text, DON'T WAIT. HAVE RIDE HOME.

He sighed, finally feeling a sense of relief and ecstatic in the moment.

* * *

After having what felt like the best time at the diner, Daniel's heart raced as Dean's car approached Daniel's house. As the car pulled curbside, it felt as if a flurry of freshly hatched butterflies were trying to break free from Daniel's stomach.

The car stopped.

Dean shifted it into PARK.

The two looked over at each other in silence, eyes lingering a fraction longer than expected.

Daniel looked out the window toward his home, where a sinking feeling started pulling the wings off his butterflies.

"So, I was thinking we should start rehearsing. Do you want to start tomorrow?" Dean asked, breaking the ice.

"Oh... Um, maybe," said Daniel. *Yes, of course you do!* The pit punched around. *Crap. I have a date. What do I tell him?*

"Maybe Sunday?" Not wishing to sit in front of his house for too long, a nervous feeling pulled his attention to the upper windows, expecting to see someone staring down. "I'll message you. Thanks for the ride."

"I can give you a ride any time you'd like. You know, to school, or rehearsal, or whatever. I don't live far from here." Dean's face flushed. "I mean, if you want."

"Uh, yeah. That'd be... Cool." Daniel didn't want to get out of the car, but he knew there'd be questions if anyone inside noticed him taking too long. The anxiety of it all forced him up and out of the car.

As Dean drove away, he tossed a wave Daniel's way, leaving him on the sidewalk with a belly full of dead butterflies.

I wonder if anybody saw...

With a quick glance around he stepped through the gate on the left of the house, closing it gently to minimize its typical creaks and whistles without blowing his cover. Daniel drifted toward the door adjacent to the garage, hoping he could sneak up the stairs to his room before anyone noticed.

Okay, here goes. I wonder if... He opened the side garage door.

His dad's truck's engine crackled and popped, letting Daniel know he must've just arrived home, earlier than expected.

No... The pit in his stomach resurfaced. *Okay, I just have to get upstairs...*

Still hopeful he could go unnoticed, he gently opened the door to the hallway and crept along the wall. As he passed Grandma's room, a nasally voice came from within the guest bathroom.

"Your father wants to speak to you." Cheryl's snide tone sent a cold shiver down his spine. Hers was not the voice he was expecting.

He knew the day's drama had been the topic of discussion. He imagined she played the victim. Maybe even being so out of touch to think it mostly embarrassed her and her perfect daughter.

Just another reason to give me the cold shoulder.

It seemed Cheryl looked for any excuse to belittle him since he and his brother were "dumped" on "her family" after the loss of their mom.

Daniel's pit doubled, but to her he didn't react. Keeping it cool, he stepped off to his bedroom without a word.

Making his way through, he glanced at his younger brother's face who donned a smart-ass smirk like, "*I knew it.*"

They both ignored each other as Daniel sat at his desk and waited for their father.

Menacing footsteps billowed down the hallway—the sound increasing in determination as the steps grew closer.

Until finally their father burst in, as if on a mission.

"Okay, Jacob. OUT! Daniel... We need to talk." His father said, dropping himself straight down on Daniel's bed. The room fell silent except for the sounds of Jacob exiting the room.

Once they were alone, his father said, "Son, come sit here," without much courtesy. His face showed the expressions of convicted, concerned, and confused all at once.

Daniel got up from the desk chair and awkwardly sat next to his dad—like a typical father-son scene from the movies.

"So, do you want to tell me what happened this morning?"

Daniel remained silent.

"Well, actually…" His father paused, not struggling to find the words. "I already heard all about it. What I really want to know is, why they are calling you that?"

There was no wait for a response.

Staring down at his own feet, his father continued, "Daniel. I want you to hear me…" He cleared his throat, and then in a stern, matter-of-fact tone, he said it.

"Son. Don't be gay."

Daniel's face instantly flushed red hot again. The words sucker punched his gut and stabbed his heart. Knowing there was no room to debate and nothing to be said, Daniel simply stared at the floor in disbelief.

Daniel's dad opened his mouth, then shut it. There was another pause before his mouth opened to confuse matters worse by adding, "It's a hard life."

His dad's incredulous words cut deep. It was almost like hearing the words, "Your mom has passed," all over again, eerily defeating.

Time seemed to stop as a high-pitched ring in Daniel's ears brought him back to that morning's emotions full force. He was once again caught off guard as his small world closed in on him.

Daniel's disillusionment was quickly replaced with what felt like righteous anger.

'Don't be gay'? 'It's a hard life'? How the hell would he know? You either are or you aren't, right? But it doesn't matter because—

"Dad. I'm not gay!" Daniel's voice cracked stronger than expected. "Those guys are just assholes!" He surprised himself with his tone. "Look, it's probably because they must've seen me rehearsing for the musical behind the theater, or something. I don't know. In fact, we don't know if it was even meant for me. There were lots of kids around. Cheryl just assumed the worst... As always," he said with authority.

Was he trying to convince himself or his father? He wasn't quite sure, but his desperation sounded reasonable.

"Besides, I have a date tomorrow. In fact, I was hoping I could borrow the truck?" He looked his dad in the eyes.

The room's energy immediately lightened, and Daniel sensed his words were placating his father—seeing his expression and body language shift from stern to disarmed.

"Oh. Well. Alright..." Daniel's father paused, sounding perplexed. And then, he almost instantly stood up, indicating he, too, wanted their "talk" to be over as soon as possible.

Oh, thank God. Leave.

Some residual shock alleviated. Daniel felt as if his plan had worked.

Until his dad paused, and more stern than before said, "Well, anyway... Son, remember what I said."

His father began to make his way out.

Just as he got to the bedroom door, he turned the knob a bit, looked back, and reiterated, "It's a hard life." His eyes focused hard on Daniel's, ensuring he was heard.

"I got it, Dad. Geeze."

"Oh, and one more thing. I called your coach and got you back on the team." His dad's face then looked as if a light bulb had gone off inside his head. "And, good news. I've decided I'm going to give you the truck now, too." He paused to make sure they held solid eye contact before he continued, "But, uh, I want you to give up the acting thing... Now... For good. You hear?" His eyes pierced through Daniel's.

"I'm not really asking, if you know what I mean," he added, wide eyed and direct.

And with that, he gave the knob a full twist, opened the door and walked out, slamming the door behind him.

A combination of anguish, guilt, disappointment, and somehow mild relief washed over Daniel. Terrified of what the day had turned out to be, he knew deep down his reputation remained under suspicion and it all left him feeling debilitated.

* * *

The next morning, Daniel slept in late. Even Jacob was already up and gone.

Bright sunlight beamed through the blinds waking him up to a sweaty room. Blinking his eyes open he heard the hustle and bustle of a full household. Dragging himself out of bed, his head pounded. He felt like he had been hit by a slow-moving vehicle.

What time is it? Oh, crap. I have to get ready.

Dazed and languid, he made his way to the bathroom. He turned on the light without looking at himself in the mirror. Drained, he didn't fuss over what to wear, what his hair was doing, or what he needed to do to make the day go well. Instead, he took a quick shower to try and find energy. When he finished, he grabbed his baggiest pants and shirt and left his hair mildly haphazard, defeated and uncaring—just enough to get by.

On his way downstairs he realized he missed the opportunity to make breakfast in peace, so he silently maneuvered past the kitchen entrance.

The squawks and cackles of Cheryl and Bianca from beyond the walls gave him the shudders.

He was just about to glide past Grandma's room to the garage when he heard a soft, concerned voice from the slightly ajar bedroom door.

"Daniel? Is that you?"

Nooo. His eyes closed, pausing for a moment as he took a deep breath.

"Daniel?" His grandma said his name again with such sincerity no one could have ignored it. "Hey, please come in here a minute."

"Hi, Grandma." Daniel poked his head through the doorway. "How are you doing? Sorry I didn't make breakfast. I'm in a bit of a rush... But hey, Dad finally gave me the truck. I was just about to take it out for a wash. Can I catch up with you later?" Doing his best to steer the conversation.

"Wait. This will just take a second. Please come sit here for a moment, would you?" Her face held eagerness and concern.

Daniel's feet dragged the rest of him over to her bedside.

"Sooo, what happened?"

Oh, no! They told her? I can't do this right now. Caught off guard, Daniel paused for a moment, The pit in his stomach reminded him it hadn't gone anywhere. Before he could say a word, she interrupted his thoughts.

"Did you get the part?" She asked with hopeful eyes.

What? Momentarily relieved but somehow even more confused. The pounding in his head prolonged a response until—

"Oh, um... No," he finally said. Closing his eyes he rubbed his face. "No, I didn't." He said without fully thinking it through—his gut reacted, but worse his heart twitched as if betrayed.

"Oh, no... I'm so sorry sweetie... That must have been a disappointment..." His grandma exhaled as she looked out the window. There was a long pause as they both silently stared at the rose garden.

No going back now. His father's words and the echoes of school bus laughter pounded in his skull.

A bright butterfly unexpectedly landed on a drooping bloom outside, breaking the room's silence.

"My goodness, they are beautiful." She paused for another moment. "But, Daniel, it's time—"

"I know." He sighed, slightly annoyed. "I'll get around to it, I promise. I just really have to get going—" The look on his grandma's face made it impossible for him to continue.

She waited another moment, staring at the beautiful bush sway as if dancing with the butterfly in the morning light before she looked at him.

"Daniel, you know I'm always here for you, right?"

When he didn't answer right away, she gently turned back to the roses and continued, "Do you remember why we don't just deadhead the wilted roses but the entire bush when it's time?"

Daniel didn't respond, but his body language was open.

"It's because it actually frees the shrub." She said with gentle conviction as she closed her eyes. Opening them, she continued, "Left unkempt and uncared for, the beautiful bush will develop into a floral thicket—a closed off thorny bramble, uninspired and bedraggled...

"But, well manicured and primped, it encourages the rose bush to focus its resources and efforts on new blossoms. And an exquisite cradle of gorgeous blooms will emerge alive and healthy, more beautiful and vibrant than before." Her enthusiasm beamed with pride from within.

"Daniel, I will never forget seeing how hard it was for you as a little boy to watch the perfect blooms taken from the bush. Your sweet face stunned, like I had just ruined the whole thing...

"But, when I showed you how we could gather the long-stemmed roses together, we could make a stunning bouquet." She turned to look at him. "Daniel, I taught you young that sometimes in life we do the hard things first to make way for something even more beautiful."

She reached for his hand. Her gentle touch sent a soft sensation of love directly to his heart. "I want this for you now, Daniel."

Her words couldn't have rung truer but at the same time felt impossibly heavy. His pit pummeled around, reminding him of something woven into his nature—screaming to be acknowledged.

"Daniel, you've always been different than the other boys, and it is beautiful. I just want you, too, to feel alive and free. But above all, happy—"

"I know, Grandma. Thank you." He sighed as he gently lifted her hand off his, letting go of the comforting feeling. "I'll get around to them. I will. But I really do have to go."

Without further details he left, and that time without looking back.

* * *

A cool breeze caught Daniel's free-flowing hand—outstretched and rhythmically making waves as it rushed through the air from the truck window.

Everything was moving fast.

The wheels on the open road, the setting sun, the music, and the time he was spending with a beautiful green-eyed girl on a Saturday.

"I love this song," she screamed, elated. Smiling ear to ear, her body moved, catching glimpses of him as she belted along, hitting every note. His black *Ray Bans* hid his dark brown doe eyes, giving him the mysterious edge he surmised she loved.

"I'm glad we finally got to hang," she said, as the song slowed, bringing down the energy.

"Me, too." He finally turned his head in her direction—a soft gesture he instinctively knew was overdue.

It wasn't that he hadn't enjoyed himself the entire day. It was that feeling she wanted more from him.

"Park us on Hilltop," she coyly whispered into his ear, leaning in, intently teasing—her lips as close to his ear without touching.

Stone-faced, he physically ignored her, checked the rear windows and made a lane change off the highway, revealing nothing more to her than "playing it cool" as his heart raced. Everything seemed to be moving too fast, but a quick flash at the clock revealed his senses had failed him and there was still plenty of time... Time to think more about what was headed his way.

The pounding in his chest linked with the ever-present pit rolling around in his stomach. But the more he thought about why, the more his thoughts upset him. Nervous creeping thoughts made his foot hit the gas.

As his truck sped, he felt himself and the engine rev.

"Whoa, Daniel," she said, keeping a cautious smile. Her right hand pressed into the dash, holding her steady as force thrust her back.

She's so beautiful. What is wrong with me? Desperately bargaining with himself. Forcing even that thought out of his mind, his foot slammed harder on the gas pedal.

A lustful smile caught his eye as her eyes focused on him, and he could tell she was falling further for his act. Making their way over the crest of the hill, he purposefully slowed the vehicle to a crawl— taking as much time as he could.

He pulled into a dark spot overlooking the glow of city lights and turned off the ignition.

Is this butterflies? The ache hanging out in his stomach turned into an odious knot. Trying to shake the comparison from his mind, he realized the more he understood the difference between butterflies and those knots, the worse his thoughts tormented him.

His phone chimed, breaking his thoughts and the silence. He glanced to see he had a new message from Dean. His heart leapt in his chest as he placed the phone back into his pocket.

"This is perfect," she whispered.

The car was silent except for the clicks and clunks of an unbuckling seatbelt. He sensed she was still completely unaware, or in denial, that his mood was rapidly shifting.

"The view is amazing up here. Wow, look at that," he faked, weakly trying to distract her attention outward.

She looked out the dash window and then back to him, taking off his sunglasses—which had overstayed their welcome.

Saying nothing, she leaned to kiss him, hitting the side of his cheek—just missing his mouth. Adjusting herself, she twisted, inching closer and slightly rising to reach his lips.

The uncomfortable knot in his stomach did a somersault.

Time was slow, but to him everything was moving too fast—which he knew normally shouldn't have been a problem.

Deciding he couldn't face why he felt the way he felt, and why he felt nothing for her, he simply turned, closed his eyes, made contact, and kissed her back.

ABOUT THE AUTHOR

DUSTY FACINELLI-JANISCH

A SOUTHERN CALIFORNIA NATIVE, DUSTY FACINELLI-JANISCH has been passionate about writing for as long as he can remember. For him, writing is not just a craft but a deeply healing, exciting, and rewarding art form. As a child, he was often lost in books, fully immersed in the magic of storytelling—a love that has only grown over time.

Dusty has honed his skills through college-level writing courses, where this particular story first took shape from a simple quick-write exercise assigned by his professor. He strives to create stories that resonate on a human level, evoking emotion and connection. Through his writing, he hopes readers not only enjoy the journey but also feel the depth of humanity woven into each page.

ABOUT LIONHEART GUILD, INC

LIONHEART GUILD, INC. IS A nonprofit organization dedicated to uplifting fresh voices and empowering ideals through the art of storytelling. Our mission is to cultivate TIMELESS TREASURES that reflect our *Purpose* and *Values* while providing a platform for underprivileged and underrepresented creators.

JOIN THE MISSION OF LIONHEART GUILD, INC.

At Lionheart Guild, Inc., we believe in the power of storytelling to transform lives. Our nonprofit is dedicated to **amplifying fresh voices** and **empowering underrepresented creators**, providing them with the platform and support they need to share their stories with the world.

Through our bi-annual anthologies, we are raising funds to build the **Read & Retreat Center**—a sanctuary for creativity, learning, and community. Every purchase, donation, and volunteer effort brings us closer to making this dream a reality.

We have **501(c)(3) public charity status**, and **your support will make a lasting impact**. Whether you donate, spread the word, or lend your time and talents, you are helping to shape a future where **stories that matter are heard**.

Join us today!

Visit *www.lionheartgrouppublishing.com*, follow us on *Facebook* at *LGPublishers*, or reach out to explore volunteer opportunities. **Together, we can bring this vision to life!**